HOLY LIES

(Part One)

S K Sheridan

"The more intense has been the religion of any period and the more profound has been the dogmatic belief, the greater has been the cruelty and the worse has been the state of affairs" Bertrand Russell

Chapter One

Twenty four hours before the murder took place, Sister Veronica Angelica leaned forward over her desk, her head cocked sideways. She was editing a thrilling car chase; a scene that rode the arc of chapter fourteen in her latest crime story beautifully. Blissfully unaware of the darkness that awaited her, the only distraction hampering her creation of a suitable climax was the incessant hammering from next door.

BANG! BANG! CRASH!

She threw down her pen and thumped the desk with her fist. Saints preserve her, did those builders not realise she only had twenty minutes before afternoon prayers began? How a nun was expected to write a book under these conditions she did not know. Aware that her trusted friend and proof reader, Sister Agnes Claire, was keen to see the finished manuscript, Sister Veronica's had an insatiable desire to finish it, but those builders had been pounding away at the extension to the youth hostel since well before morning prayers. It was terribly off-putting. While extra room at the busy hostel was much needed, and she should know because she worked there three days a week, at this rate she was going to have to wait until after evening mass to finish the chapter. Which was *such* a shame as she had been so looking forward to penning the moment Father Dominic discovered his housekeeper's body in the back of a burnt out car.

Her train of thought now disrupted, Sister Veronica squinted through the window at the vibrant street life of London's Soho Square Gardens, her sharp green eyes taking in the sunbathers on the fenced in square of patchy grass, the smiling couples walking hand in hand, the Japanese tourists with their cameras and the troop of Hare Krishna followers weaving a lively passage through everyone else. All the activity took place theatre-like amid the set of a quadrangle of historic four storey buildings; the view was definitely Sister Veronica's favourite for people-watching. She felt an air of light expectancy pervading the streets, matching the warmer than usual Spring climate, and she exhaled, smiling. But the sight of a scuttling tall, brown-haired man wearing a dog collar and advancing towards her building prompted her eyebrows to lower, as she remembered who was taking afternoon prayers in the Convent of The Christian Heart that day.

Sighing, she wondered if she was the only one to dislike Father Mathers. His slippery eye contact, habit of listening at doors, and questionable comments about anyone who didn't fit his idea of middle class and above, made him an unsavoury compatriot. Yet so many of the other Sisters seemed to adore him, and his clever sermons had them talking for days. Sister Veronica knew she mustn't let on that she didn't like the man, people were too close for comfort in her world and word would get back to him. She had no plans to draw attention to herself, not after last time. It had all been most unpleasant and eyes had been on her for weeks; creeping away for murder-mystery writing had become nearly impossible.

Taking a deep breath, Sister Veronica shut her notebook and stood up. Catching sight of her reflection in the window she chuckled. Well, well, well, it looked like she'd put on a few more pounds. She saw that some wisps of her grey hair, pulled back in a sensible bun that morning, had come loose and hung round her face. For a moment she was transported back to her childhood, when, despite her mother's best efforts to tame them, locks of her then red hair had continually escaped as she galloped through the fields of her parent's Sussex farm. Memories of the terrible moment she'd found out her adored parents weren't all that they seemed flashed by, and her heart began its usual pounding.

Feeling her eyes moisten, she shook her head. Now now, we'll have none of that, thank you, she told herself. Good grief, there's no time for baby tears. Not when that priest's mutterings have to be endured with passable grace.

Smoothing down her long tweed skirt and wishing her supposedly loose fitting blouse wasn't pinching quite so tightly, Sister Veronica opened her bedroom door. Now keep that temper of yours under control, she told herself sternly, stepping out into the bare corridor. Even if he says the most trying things, don't react. No trouble, not again. It makes writing so very difficult, and that just won't do. Kneel quietly, reflect on your vows, pray for the poor and think of how best to end the chapter.

Adopting her customary rolling gait, and heading through the double doors and towards the staircase, Sister Veronica brushed her blouse downwards in case any stray crumbs had stayed behind after her early-afternoon snack. Custard Creams did aid the writing process, she found. As she lumbered slowly down the stairs, she could hear bedroom doors opening and closing, a variety of footsteps getting louder behind her; the motley crew of seven other Sisters who shared life in the Convent were also on their way.

Sister Veronica was just reflecting on how, being two floors up, she did quite a lot of exercise on a daily basis, what with all the meal times and prayers and masses held on the ground floor, when she saw a bob of bright blonde hair through the window of the fire door on the first floor.

"Oh dash," she murmured, as the door swung open, and a young lady fell in to step with her.

"Alright Sister Veronica?" The young lady said, her husky South London accent still unfamiliar within the convent walls; not grating exactly - almost exotic - a reminder of other worlds and lives. Her eyes sought out the nun's; the startling keenness and drive in them contrasting with the customary dissociation Sister Veronica saw in many of her Sisters' eyes.

"Oh hello Melissa, what a pleasant surprise," Sister Veronica said, giving the young journalist a once over. Apart from exchanging pleasantries at mealtimes, she'd so far successfully avoided talking to this attractive imposter who'd burst into their quiet religious life three days ago. She had to look upwards to take in the girl's angular, bronzed face with its wide green eyes, which was framed by a bob of wavy dyed blonde hair smattered with fading pink highlights. Sister Veronica instinctively pulled her spine in, drawing herself up to her maximum possible height of five feet three inches, then glanced over at Melissa to see if she'd gained anything on her.

Typically, it had been Father Mathers who, when Women of the World Magazine emailed him asking if he knew any Sisters who would be happy to have a reporter living with them for a week to find out "what life was really like as a nun", had persuaded Mother Superior that it would be a sensible idea to allow the journalist to stay at the convent.

Another way of building good community links, he'd said. Maybe he'd seen a photo of Melissa Carlton prior to his enthusiasm, Sister Veronica had speculated, before pushing the thought into the very private "not for public consumption" section of her brain.

Melissa threw Sister Veronica a wide smile, flashing a row of large white teeth, a wide gap between the front two.

"Prayer time is so peaceful isn't it?" The girl said. Yes, still a girl, Sister Veronica was sure she couldn't be a day over twenty six. "I don't often get a chance to stop and think in my normal life, but I've thought more over the last few days than I have all year."

"Yes. Quite." Sister Veronica did indeed find prayers and mass very peaceful times. She fervently believed in a higher power greater than all humankind, but Father Mather's subtly prejudiced sermons made her brain overheat, and she didn't think God would mind if she tuned those bits out in favour of ruminating on her next chapter. Also after having been a Sister for over thirty eight years, which was arguably a long time for anyone to enjoy near-constant meditation on Catholic dogma and discipline, Vatican II and the uproarious news events that had dogged the Roman Catholic Church throughout the twenty first century, Sister Veronica couldn't help but see a chasm-like difference between what she sensed was there spiritually, and the human-made world of religion; which at times – and she was sorry but this was the truth - was nothing but trouble. She hadn't lost her faith, no, not at all. The fact was she'd developed her own simple belief, a pact of love between the greater power of the multiverse and herself, and that was who she prayed to. The militant Catholic rule-keepers and dogma enthusiasts who loved to tell people they were wrong all the time had to be borne with a detached patience. The problem was, as Sister Veronica frequently reflected, she wasn't very good at detached patience and constantly had to bite down the urge to tell them exactly what she thought of them.

"I'm glad I've caught you actually," Melissa said, stopping and waiting at the bottom of the staircase for Sister Veronica to roll down the last few steps. "I've been hoping we could arrange to have a quick chat at some point, whenever suits you really?"

Sister Veronica Angelica sighed inwardly. She'd had an inkling this question was coming; over the last few days she'd watched four of her other Sisters peel off from communal activities to have nice cosy chats with Melissa in the garden or the lobby.

"Alright," she replied, puffing a bit as she reached the ground floor, the heavy wooden cross she wore round her neck swinging from side to side. "How about during reading time, before dinner? I'll have to check with Mother Superior but I don't think she'll mind. We can take a walk in the garden, perhaps". Sister Veronica had no intention of going up all those stairs to her room again, not until after evening prayers.

"Perfect, that works well for me," Melissa's eyes darted around, watching the nuns descend the stairs one by one and head for the chapel.

"Right, then." Sister Veronica waited by the stairs, hoping that now she'd succumbed to Melissa's wishes, the young journalist would leave her alone. She'd become so used to the quietness in the convent that she found talking too much within its walls intrusive, especially to people she hardly knew. It was different next door in the youth hostel of course, that was a place designed for socialising; the atmosphere was alive and dynamic, and chatting was a necessary part of that. But here in the convent the near silence was sacred.

Melissa seemed to get the hint, and smiled before walking off. But then she stopped and turned.

"You won't forget, will you?" She asked, her eyes betraying her, a hint of something in them suddenly – now what was it - desperation? Fear? Sister Veronica caught her breath in astonishment, then shook her head. If the girl's presence in the convent held a meaning beyond the act of journalism, she had no intention of finding out what it was. Any hint of trouble, as far as she was concerned, could stay very far away from her indeed.

Dawdling in the stairwell to give Melissa a good head start into the chapel, she nodded to the last of her comrades to descend the stairs; Sister Maria, a shy novice who was still in the first flush of religious ideation.

"Are you coming, Sister?" Sister Maria peered at her anxiously. "We don't want to be late".

"I'm on my way, Sister. Just resting my sore knee for a minute, you know how it plays up. You go on and I'll follow." Sister Veronica nodded and ushered the novice away with her hands. She was fond of Sister Maria, and wondered, vaguely, why the enthusiastic young novice was the last one down to prayers when she was usually one of the first.

Her mind slipped back to her chapter, she knew there was an idea there just waiting to be teased to the surface. All she needed was a bit of peace to encourage it and she fully intended to kneel near the back, as this was her best thinking place. Watching Sister Maria's back view disappear, she walked slowly towards the chapel, past the kitchen door that was pulled to. A smell of boiled milk from lunchtime's rice pudding hung in the air, mingling with the sharp odours of cleaning products. From inside the kitchen came a low murmuring – two voices. One was a man's voice. Father Mathers, she thought, surprised. Why isn't he already in chapel? And who's he talking to? Sister Veronica didn't mean to listen, not really. It was her bad knee that made her slow down to a halt and sway towards the door.

"No I haven't done it yet. You'll have to give me more time." Father Mathers spat each word out in low staccato.

Someone must have responded although Sister Veronica couldn't hear what was being said or who was saying it. She held her breath.

"I've promised you haven't I? Now I really must go, or they'll wonder where I am". He sounded agitated, a far cry from his usual smooth persona. There was the sound of a chair scraping backwards.

With unusual speed, Sister Veronica lunged towards the chapel, dropping heavily into the nearest pew, the impact making her wince. She buried her head in her hands. Numb shock gave way to an angry, rising heat. What was that foolish priest up to? Fighting the instinct to immediately report what she'd heard to Mother Superior or even announce it to the assembled nuns, she remembered her promise to herself to remain inconspicuous and keep out of trouble.

The chapel, the largest ground floor room in their historic building, had originally been used as a library for the Duke of Sussex. Normally, Sister Veronica liked to imagine the layers of contemplation and reflection that had taken place within its walls over the changing centuries. She knew that King Charles II had the building constructed for his friend, the Duke, in 1677, when Soho Square was quite the fashionable place for aristocracy to live. Now, maintained by Westminster City Council, the building was stripped of any grandeur inside, which Sister Veronica was glad about as she couldn't abide fancy airs and graces. She wholeheartedly believed in her vow of poverty which didn't mean – as a few lay people seemed to think – that religious folk promised to live in abject destitution. It was more about all possessions belonging with equal weight to each member of the community, and living with gratitude and modesty; Sister Veronica suspected that this Western fascination with capitalism could learn a thing or two from it.

But there was no time for historical rumination today, it was all she could do to slow her breaths and hope that the pulsating angry heat in her head and heart wasn't obvious. As she grasped the wooden pew in front for strength, a whoosh of air beside her and the loud tones that followed announced Father Mather's arrival.

"Good Sisters," he projected his educated – now calm - tones around the room. "Let us bow our heads in prayer as we ask for the grace to answer your call with obedience and love".

After a few minutes of furious prayer for the continued protection and sanctity of her convent in the face of all wrongdoing, Sister Veronica peered through her fingers and allowed herself a quick glance around. Sister Maria, right at the front, was looking up with no doubt rapt attention at Father Mathers, who now stood behind the altar, his arms spread beneficently outwards, his eyes closing. His robes hung slickly around him and his carefully parted hair remained unruffled. Sister Veronica added "good actor" to her list of his character traits. Who were you just talking to? Sister Veronica asked him silently. What haven't you done yet? What have you promised? She couldn't and wouldn't look at the man for long in case her thoughts were so loud they drew his attention to her, so she let her hidden gaze pan sideways.

Behind Sister Maria, knelt Sister Agnes Claire, Sister Veronica's best friend at the convent. Her shoulders were sagging, and Sister Veronica suspected that her friend's rheumatism had been keeping her up again so she said a quick prayer, asking for Sister Agnes's pain be taken away. The cold British climate was a far cry from her friend's birth place of Kerala state in southwestern India, and rheumatic pain had dogged her since her arrival in London eighteen years previously. Sister Veronica wondered whether to relay the overheard conversation to Sister Agnes at some point.

Turning her head a fraction to the right, she saw Melissa kneeling further down her pew, the fear in her eyes now gone but the look on her face unreadable as she stared straight ahead. On the other side of Melissa, was Mother Superior, Sister Julia Augusta. Her eyes were closed and her lined face as sternly pious as usual. Mother Superior always arrived fifteen minutes before every prayer session and mass, typically sinking to her knees with histrionic zeal and staying rigidly still until ten minutes after each session had finished. Sister Veronica felt this exaggerated obeisance to the powers that be might be slightly over doing it, but who was she to comment. Mother Superior had been at the convent for forty three years and was the longest practising Sister, yet no one knew much about her at all. Discussing one's previous life wasn't encouraged as it apparently distracted a nun from fully giving herself over to God, and each Sister adhered to this in greater or lesser ways; some were naturally more open, and everyone knew everything about jolly Sister Catherine's former life and was all the better for it, in Sister Veronica's opinion.

Sister Catherine, still a relative newcomer by convent standards had arrived from Australia the year before. A ruddy faced natural extrovert, she loved to talk and often kept Sister Veronica entertained with tales from her parent's outback farm during mealtimes. Sister Veronica couldn't see her or her two other Sisters, they must be kneeling in the pews behind her and she couldn't very well turn her head round to stare, which was vexing as she liked to keep an eye on everything that was going on.

On second thoughts, it was probably for the best as the last thing she wanted to do was make eye contact with Sister Irene, whose role as Assistant Superior made her second in command at the convent. Although the nuns elected Mother and Assistant Superiors every five years, and the nuns undertaking these roles were still meant to be equals to the rest of the Sisters in the convent, Sister Veronica often suspected that Sister Irene hadn't received that important bit of information. A ferocious rule-keeper and dogma enthusiast, Sister Irene looked sourly on Sister Veronica's mild rebellious tendencies to think for herself and took every opportunity to get her in trouble. She must be sitting with old Sister Anastasia, who tended to drift off during longer masses, and Sister Mary Pemii who was in the midst of a six month visit from a Convent of the Christian Heart in Nigeria.

Risking a peek towards Father Mathers, she saw the priest's eyes were now wide open. He was staring straight at her, a strange look on his face. She had a sudden thought that he'd seen her walking away from the kitchen and had realised she'd overheard his conversation. Maybe she'd been too slow, maybe her footsteps had been too loud. Intentionally keeping her face as mild and blank as possible, her heart rate quickened and a small thrill of rage ricocheted through her. Why should she be feeling guilty for walking through her own home? It wasn't right. It wouldn't do at all. She bowed her head downwards, and said a prayer for all those with deceitful intent, asking that they may live with honesty and without guile.

After several minutes, she raised her eyes. Father Mathers eyes had closed again, his hands pressed together as though in deep prayer.

Now calm down, she counselled herself. The angry heat inside her ebbed a bit, and Sister Veronica wondered whether she'd read more into the encounter than was really there. Was it possible that she'd let her personal dislike for

Father Mathers colour her judgment? It wouldn't be the first time. Perhaps it was an innocent promise not yet fulfilled, such as paying the gardener, or counselling a seminarian, it wouldn't surprise her if it was that tall young fair-haired trainee she'd seen trailing after him recently; those two had developed an unusually close bond. Relaxing a little, she heard the front door click into place. Clearly, whoever he'd been speaking to had just left.

Suddenly the whole peculiar encounter seemed surreal and she felt a little foolish. She didn't like Father Mathers, that was for sure. The problem with clericalism was that it changed some people for the worse. If they didn't live their lives from love and cut themselves off too much from the comfort of human contact it dehumanised them; they became cold, selfish, sometimes unpleasant. She'd seen it happen many times, and Father Mathers fitted the bill perfectly. No one could forget the awful saga with Father Cuthbert; the courts had found him guilty of molesting three altar boys and the shame it brought on the Diocese of Westminster was still tangible. Word among the religious folk was that Cardinal Moore was planning a series of targeted visits around Westminster with the press in tow.

While Sister Veronica didn't hold with much of the sensationalist reporting that went on nowadays, she felt anything that raised the profile of good, hardworking priests and nuns would be beneficial.

She sighed. She'd written enough crime fiction – in secret of course, entirely unpublished more's the pity – to know that basing an indictment on one overheard conversation alone was ridiculous. The best thing, she decided, was to ignore the man. She'd forget she ever heard anything and carry on as before. No need to tell Sister Agnes about her experience. It was probably nothing anyway, she told herself. Probably nothing at all.

Closing her eyes, she visualised the next events in her chapter, the car chase, the crash, the burnt out wreckage, the housekeeper's body. She imagined Sister Agnes's delight and absorption while reading it. Her mind's eye panned slowly onto the housekeeper's face. Suddenly it changed, metamorphosing into Father Mather's face. His eyes were open, staring at her, a smirk twisting his bulbous features. She shivered and her right hand clasped firmly around her wooden cross.

Chapter 2

Clearing away the debris from breakfast time, Jamie Markham rolled up his sleeves; yesterday's warm air had turned stickily humid. His bare wrists bore the giant scars from last year's suicide attempt; violent white slashes criss-crossed with the lifesaving marks of the surgeon's stitches – a permanent reminder of the night he'd lacerated his arms with the broken glass of a wine bottle. He didn't like people looking at them, but there was no one else nearby; all the other hostel guests had already upped and left the room, most of them already out of the building, doing whatever it was they did during the day.

Cursing the students – and they were mainly students or backpackers with the exception of the old hippie, Jon Barrow - for the bloody mess they made every mealtime, (they ate like pigs in his opinion), Jamie felt a pang of satisfaction as he guided each crumb, fragment of egg shell, crust and apple core into a neat pile at the edge of the table. Using his carefully rinsed dish cloth for guidance, he swiped the pile into his hand with mathematical precision, successfully aiming every piece for the centre of his palm with no collateral damage falling to the floor. He admired his own dexterity, then hated himself for admiring it.

Purposefully not looking through the window at the rubble of bricks messing up the garden, Jamie realised that the throbbing in his head had already eased; in fact it had started to wane the minute he'd read the note he'd found on the doormat at seven that morning written in perfect copperplate swirls; "Builders not coming today, been called to an emergency, should be back over the next couple of days. God bless, Sister Julia". The incessant bloody banging that had marked each day for two weeks as the workmen knocked down an old wall outside had physically hurt his brain. Since his mother had gone hysterical in the hospital after seeing the stitches criss-crossing his lacerated wrists for the first time, Jamie's thoughts had become physically painful, and each blow of the builders' sledgehammers magnified this pain. Keeping busy was a good distraction from this, and quietness was a balm.

Walking into the kitchen to deposit his handful into the food waste bin, Jamie saw Mark and the new French girl Celine chatting near the door to the dining room. They were standing very close together. Celine's low top revealed a generous portion of her firm, tanned breasts and Jamie wished it was him talking to her instead of Mark.

Turning away before they saw him, Jamie brought his attention back to today's main task. He'd identified which of the nuns from next door's convent he was going to tell his secret to – he'd chosen that large-faced one Sister Veronica as she reminded him of his grandmother, she actually listened when he talked, she didn't just disengage from people in the sanctimonious way some of the other Sisters did – now he just needed to work out how and when to orchestrate the conversation. He'd have to choose a moment when her friend, that old busy body Father John, wasn't around. They usually turned up within an hour of each other.

It was imperative that he got the conditions just right, everything he wanted to do and all the action he wanted to take, depended on Sister Veronica's help. He knew that what had happened to him all those years ago wasn't right, but he still found it very difficult to talk about. But he must, he must. The bottled up anger was killing him.

It had been an impulse to arrange a stay at the Catholic Youth Hostel two months previously. Jamie knew a connection to Westminster Diocese was important to establish if he was going to achieve what he wanted to, but he'd struggled to know how to initiate it. Googling the area, he'd come across the Convent of the Christian Heart and the hostel they ran. A short phone call later, Jamie found himself on the train from Sidcup, the sleepy Kent suburb where his mum lived, to London's Victoria Station the next day, his modest savings transferred to his current account. He was an artist, he'd said to the nuns who'd welcomed him, studying at Kensington College of Art and Design, and needed somewhere to stay. Which wasn't a complete lie, was it? His cover story held many elements of truth. He'd been to art college for a year and seven months, albeit in Bromley not Kensington. The suicide attempt and its aftermath had ground his fine art project on Impressions of Horror to an abrupt halt, but the nuns didn't need to know that detail. Anyway, he knew what he had to do here was more important than creating coagulating blood effects on canvas with acrylic paint. He'd found his true calling, and by following it he would be repairing some of the damage done to him.

Just thinking about the importance of his plan caused Jamie's heart to beat faster, dizziness to flood his brain. He'd been prone to panic attacks since he'd read that letter two months ago, and he hated himself for being so weak. Leaning against the sink, he tried to regulate his breaths, and commended himself for the calm feeling that washed through his body. Then he hated himself for his own vanity. Then he hated all the people; the priests, his mother, his fucking teachers, who'd drip-fed him the idea that vanity, that anything for that matter, was a sin. Fucking Catholic bullshit. Jamie knew from experience that Catholicism was a cult, and that he was one of its victims. But not for much longer.

The sight of a knife covered in strawberry jam lying on a plate nearby jolted his increasingly obsessive mind. He mustn't let his standards slip; he'd felt honoured when Sister Catherine, after guessing that he was struggling with money, had suggested he swap his housekeeping abilities for a vastly reduced room fee. He washed up the remaining breakfast clutter with a thoroughness Sister Veronica had commended on many occasions. The two of them had become quite close, Jamie thought. He'd often found her staring at him intently, not unkindly, just with an absorbed interest, and he'd come to the conclusion that maybe he reminded her of a brother or nephew from long ago.

Drying each bowl, side plate, spoon and knife until any hint of moisture had been meticulously removed, Jamie heard voices, a carefree laugh – Celine's, he thought – then the opening and closing of the front door. The last of the hostel's guests had left. He paused, realising Mark and Celine had left together. Then he exhaled, relieved at the sudden solitude. It was Sister Veronica's day to visit the hostel, Jamie had memorised her timetable a couple of weeks ago. Always a stickler for punctuality, she would arrive at half past three on the dot, armed with ingredients for today's tea time cake. He would offer to help her make it. It would be the perfect time for him to disclose his secret to her, before the hustle and bustle of the returning rabble ruined their time together.

A scraping noise in the backyard jolted him from his thoughts. What was that? Probably a bird or a cat. There was enough rubbish out there these days to entertain a whole army of bored wildlife. A tepid breeze wafted over his arms. He must have left the back door open, he thought.

He'd got into the habit of doing that due to those bloody builders usually going in and out all day. Placing the last gleaming knife carefully in the correct section in the cutlery drawer, Jamie turned towards the utility room.

Chapter Three

Sister Veronica tucked her carrier bag under her arm and clutched the banister. It was half past two and a muggy air was pervading the convent. Dressed for the heat in her lightest skirt and shirt, she stomped down the stairs a little louder than was necessary. She wouldn't have admitted to this for one minute, but combined with her tired agitation was a sense of aliveness; a part of her that had been asleep for years had woken up. It had been that conversation yesterday with the girl Melissa that had done it, on top of yesterday's strange goings on. What with having a penchant for creating mysteries through writing, there was something curiously thrilling about being involved with something unexplained oneself.

At first, sitting in the garden with the young journalist in the sultry afternoon sun, Sister Veronica had been impatient. She'd wanted to get the meeting done and over with as soon as possible; she missed the peace that writing gave her. The girl was likeable enough, even if she did have a rather loose dress sense. There was something elegant about the way she carried herself, and it must have taken some pluckiness to have immersed herself in the unique convent setting, after all it was not something that was usually possible for outsiders. But she didn't really see what either party could gain from what was sure to be a superficial chat, what could she possibly say that would interest her? They'd both chosen different life paths, they had vastly different ways of living, why couldn't they just both get on with going about their business, instead of pretending that some cultural value would emerge from a ten minute interaction? Remember your vows, Veronica, she told herself. For once just be obedient without making such a fuss.

Melissa had stared out over the small yellowing lawn for a good few seconds. The scent of dry grass had hung around them, as still as the air. The girl had sat straight backed, a beaded kaftan flowing over her bronzed limbs, her slim legs - clad in long white leggings - neatly crossed. Sister Veronica had found herself staring at the girl's sandals, which were dark bronze in colour with light and dark beads threaded over the straps. They were strangely fascinating. But she'd remembered something her mother had told her many years ago, that it was rude to stare at someone's shoes as it made you come across as disdainful, so she forced her gaze away and adopted a look of patient beneficence until the girl was ready to talk.

"Sister Veronica," Melissa had begun in her gravelly tones. "Thank you so much for taking the time to talk to me, I really do appreciate it. If you feel comfortable with this, could you tell me a bit about what led up to your decision to enter a convent?"

With an internal sigh, this was exactly the sort of question she'd predicted Melissa would ask, Sister Veronica elaborated on how she was brought up in a devout Catholic family, how she'd always felt an affinity with the Sisters who'd taught her in school, and how she'd felt called to be a nun because she felt most herself when she was at one with God. There was no point explaining to the girl about how over the years she'd started questioning the way some parts of the Catholic Church worked, and that now she'd made peace with her own private relationship with God, or love or the universe, or whatever you wanted to call it. Goodness knows the Church had had enough bad press recently, and the last thing it needed was some young journalist twisting her words to sell magazines. And there was absolutely no way she would ever tell Melissa about the awful thing that had happened when she was thirteen, and that part of her decision to become a nun was driven by guilt.

Melissa had pulled out a shiny notebook and had written in large swirly writing while she talked.

"Do you mind if I ask if you ever considered getting married or starting a family, before you became a nun?" The girl's eyes had sharpened as she asked this question.

Sister Veronica smiled. If the girl was hoping for some juicy gossip she certainly wouldn't be getting any.

"My dear," she'd replied, pulling herself up. "Women who choose to be nuns are still human. Of course we have past lives, some of us have fallen in love with men before, or even had relationships before we took our vows. To know how to love is one of the greatest assets of being a nun. But the trick is knowing that *after* one takes one's vows, one will be able to direct that love in other ways, such as working with the community, which is one of my favourite things to do, why I spend so much time in the hostel next door. My vows of chastity, obedience and poverty are very important to me and I have always kept them, it is my pleasure to do so". Except obedience, she added to herself. On the odd occasion. After all, to err is human, to forgive is divine.

"It's just…" Melissa began, then stopped. Why did the girl suddenly look troubled? Was she thinking of becoming a nun, and didn't know if she could be celibate? From the way she'd seen Father Mather's young protégé, Father Adams, staring at Melissa, and from the look she'd given him in return, Sister Veronica felt that whatever the girl's future career involved it certainly wasn't celibacy.

"Yes?" Sister Veronica asked gently, half expecting a confession of some sort.

"There is something else I want to ask you actually," In an instant, Melissa seemed to shrink; instead of a glamorous journalist, Sister Veronica suddenly saw a scared child in front of her. "But…"

"Ask me anything you like," Sister Veronica chuckled. "I may be a nun, but I can assure you I'm rarely shocked by anything these days."

"No it's not that," Melissa bit her little finger nail. "It's just, I don't know if I'm allowed to talk to you about this. I think I better check with my, um, boss, before I ask you."

"That's absolutely fine, Melissa. Come and find me whenever you're ready and we can continue the conversation." Sister Veronica stared at the girl, puzzled. Well, this was unexpected. There was clearly something disturbing her but what on earth could that be? Seeing someone so affected tugged exasperatingly at her heart. It was the vulnerability, it made her want to care for the person, to protect them from the world. Their pain became her pain. She was sure a psychologist would have a field day with this, given her own teenage experiences. But no psychologist would ever get the chance, she was sure of that.

Melissa shook her head a little, a dazed expression on her face.

"Thank you," she said, standing up, and regaining some of her composure. "You've been very kind. I'll get back to you as soon as I can, when I've had a word with my editor." The dry grass had scratched Sister Veronica's ankles as she rose to follow her.

Yesterday, this conversation had seemed intriguing, to the point where Sister Veronica had lost valuable sleeping hours mulling it over. But today it felt vexing. Tantalising snip bits just wouldn't do. For goodness sake, she'd nearly fallen asleep during morning prayers, and lunchtime sitting next to Sister Catherine had been a veritable struggle. On top of that, was the intolerably relentless heat. Running the back of her hand across her damp forehead, she finally arrived on the ground floor and trudged towards the kitchen.

Thankfully, there was no one else there. She could hear murmurings from the garden; Sisters Maria and Mary were probably tending to the sparse beds of flowers. Sometimes they wheeled Sister Anastasia outside. Although nearly blind now, Sister Anastasia did enjoy being in the sun. A look of peace would come over her as she drifted off. She was the last of the nuns to continue wearing her dark blue habit, wispy strands of hair escaping from its neat folds. Sister

Veronica was glad she'd taken hers off twenty years ago, when given the choice. Wearing it in this humidity would have been too much. She hoped Sister Agnes was out in the garden too, the heat would do her rheumatism no end of good.

Dumping her carrier bag on the counter, she retrieved a packet of Custard Creams from the snack cupboard. Crunching through them, she ferreted around for today's cake ingredients. She wasn't in the right frame of mind for the coffee and walnut one, todays would be a plain jam sponge.

As she finished shoving the last of her requirements into her bag, the sound of the door creaking made her turn.

"Ah. Sister Irene."

"Hello, Sister. I see you found the Custard Creams again." Sister Irene looked down her nose at the empty packet, before whisking it away to the recycling bin. "Why not try an apple next time?"

Sister Veronica stopped what she was doing and peered up at the tall, sour-faced nun, who was now making a show of wiping crumbs from the kitchen worktop. For heaven's sake, there were better things she could be doing with her afternoon than batting away minor affronts. Sister Irene could never let a meeting between them pass without getting some digs in. She could be rude in such polite ways that she sometimes left her unsuspecting targets emotionally bruised but bewildered as to exactly what had happened. Mark her words, Sister Veronica had witnessed it happening, and Sister Irene a woman of the cloth. She should be ashamed of herself.

"Oh I don't think so, Sister. The peel always gets stuck in my teeth". She glanced indiscreetly at the kitchen clock. "Now if you'll excuse me I'm off to the youth hostel." Sister Veronica picked up her bag.

"Going to see that strange creature, Jamie, are you?" Sister Irene asked, her eyes widening a fraction.

"I'm sure I'll see young Jamie while I'm there, yes." Sister Veronica replied. "And I don't think he's strange, just a little damaged by something. You can see it in his eyes". She wasn't going to let on that Jamie fascinated her. The way he seemed to live inside his head, his brooding countenance, his pained eyes. She'd taken to studying him carefully, and he was dangerously close to becoming a character in her book.

"Well you'd know, I'm sure." Sister Irene's eyes flared. What on earth did she mean by that? "Have a good afternoon, Sister. Happy baking." A self-satisfied smile flickered across her lips.

At half past three on the dot, trying to evacuate cantankerous thoughts about Sister Irene, Sister Veronica walked out of the convent, pulling the front door shut behind her with a bang. Emerging from the stone porch and glancing left and right, she satisfied herself that Father Mathers was not about. The last thing she wanted to do was bump in to him today. She was looking forward to her friend Father John's arrival at the hostel; he could always be counted on to knock at the door around half past four every weekday afternoon. Now at least with him there was a chance of sane conversation. And unlike Sister Irene, he didn't view poor Jamie as strange. If anything, he seemed rather protective over the boy. The students tended to arrive back in dribs and drabs soon after Father John's appearance, all hungry and all expecting cake. Sister

Veronica enjoyed their vibrancy; they were like balls in a pinball machine, so carefree and spontaneous.

A yellowing atmosphere pervaded Soho Square Gardens. The people on the grass had lost the happy countenance of yesterday's sun-worshippers; today's seemed listless, all silently still as though in a tableau of depression.

Although she had a key to the hostel, she always felt it was polite to knock, just in case she took Jamie by surprise. He was such a fragile looking thing she didn't want to startle him, and he seemed to have taken to her for some reason, always striking up stilted conversations.

Arriving outside the faded white door, she rapped loudly three times. The usual scurrying footsteps did not materialise. She tried again, then rummaged for the key.

The door clicked open. It was strangely quiet. Perhaps Jamie was having a lie down, or maybe he'd popped out to the shops. She hoped he had, it would do him good to get out more.

"Hello?" Sister Veronica called, heaving her bag of goods inside and shutting the door behind her. "Jamie, are you there?"

No answer. Well, she'd make a start anyway.

As she unpacked the jar of jam, eggs, flour and butter on to the kitchen counter, a warm breeze wafted her long skirt to and fro. Perhaps Jamie had left the back door open. Silly boy. Maybe where he hailed from in Kent it was safe enough to leave doors open when no one was in, but in London's West End it certainly wasn't.

Wandering through to the utility room she saw that the back door was indeed wide open. Hmm. She'd have to have a word with him about that.

She stopped, electrocuted by shock.

Through the open door she could see a pair of feet lying very still. They had Jamie's trainers on.

She leaned forward to look.

Jamie Markham lay amid the builders' rubble in the backyard, a pool of redness oozing out around his head. Congealed blood covered his matted brown hair, and his skull was crushed at the side.

Sister Veronica staggered back in shock. Her stomach twisted, and for a moment she wondered whether she was going to vomit.

After minutes that could have been hours, she forced herself to come to her senses, un-rooting herself from the lino tiles.

Police. She must call the police. Everyone who came to stay in the hostel had mobile phones these days, so there was only an old broken pay phone in the corner of the living room. She must go back to the convent.

RAT-A-TAT-TAT!

The door knocker hammered as she approached the door from this inside.

"Who is it?" She called. She didn't recognise her voice, it was high, brittle.

"Father Mathers," the voice on the other side snapped in reply. "Do please hurry up and open the door, good Sister. It's starting to rain."

Chapter Four

"What?" Sister Veronica whispered. The world had turned surreal.

RAT-A-TAT-TAT-TAT-TAT

"Open this door, please! We're getting soaked." Father Mathers' shout swam with righteous petulance.

There's a chance this man can help, Sister Veronica told herself as she fumbled with the Chubb lock, her fingers as helpful as deadweight's. It doesn't matter if you like him or not, he can help. He must be able to help.

A hand grabbed the door after she released the lock, pulling it wide open.

There in front of her stood Father Mathers, very damp, his face contorting from irritation to magnanimity. Next to him, smoothly dressed in black with the white on his dog collar shining, was Cardinal Moore, also dripping, his eyes immediately penetrating into Sister Veronica's glazed ones. During previous rare meetings, she'd always been fascinated by how the Cardinal's hawk eyes contrasted with his otherwise innocent baby-face. He had a powerful air about him, no doubt about that; something about his height gave him a commanding appearance. Control had never been a quality near the top of Sister Veronica's favourite character trait list. But there was no time to think of that now.

"Well, aren't you going to ask us in, Sister?" Father Mathers laughed, as though they'd arrived at a jolly birthday party and the door had been opened by a shy child. "His Eminence and I were just chatting about how wonderful a cup of tea would taste. Could you possibly let us come in to dry off a bit, and perhaps, er, put the kettle on?"

"Your Eminence. Father Mathers," Sister Veronica said, drawing herself up, shaking. Come on Veronica, she told herself. Get a dashed grip.

"Come quickly. Something terrible has happened," she said. No other words were possible.

Seconds later, they all stood in the back garden, staring at the broken body that used to house Jamie Markham.

Sister Veronica wondered at the heinous things some people were capable of. She'd seen dead bodies before of course, the first two being her own mother and father. Well, the man who she called her father, who she'd learnt in the cruellest way that day when she was thirteen, wasn't biologically related to her at all. She'd sat with parishioners as they took their last breaths, sometimes she'd been the only person there to ease them into the next dimension of being. And there was a next dimension, she could feel it. Consciousness was not just chemicals that disappeared when the heart stopped beating, no matter what New Scientist articles claimed, and mark her words she'd read a few in the dentists waiting room. It was all very well banging on about quarks and tetra quarks, and that nothing was there before the Big Bang, but if science was to be considered alongside the Biblical explanations for existence, then what made these quarks? What allowed there to be nothing before there was something? The next experience of life may not be the patriarchal set up purported by tradition, but it was there alright.

But why, why, why would anyone do this to Jamie? Why? She'd noticed the scars on his wrists before, although he'd taken pains to hide them. Knew he had a tortured past, that he must have tried to kill himself. She'd never asked him about it, presumed he'd tell her if he wanted to. But he hadn't killed himself. He'd survived and gone on, and now someone had taken that new effort at life away from him. Her eyes moistened but she didn't care. There was no shame at mourning this horror, this unnecessary extinction of young life. Why does suffering exist?

"Appalling." Cardinal Moore said, his words cutting across her nightmarish reverie. Father Mathers, she saw, had frozen. "This is utterly appalling."

"Yes," Sister Veronica agreed quietly. "It is."

"And on Church run property," the Cardinal glared. Sister Veronica's eyes snapped round to lazer into his.

"Pardon, Your Eminence? Surely the tragedy here is the loss of Jamie's life. I was just on the way to call the police when - "

"No. No police, Sister. Not yet. This is a Church matter, and must be dealt with by Canonical Law first, the highest law, one that comes before and above civil law."

Sister Veronica shook her head frantically.

"But - " she began.

"And yes of course the tragedy here is the poor boy's loss of life. Of course it is, God rest his soul." The Cardinal's words severed hers. "If you want justice served here as much as I do, we must turn the matter over to God, surely you can see that? Sadly murder comes under *graviora delicta,* the most serious of all sins investigated under Canon Law. The ultimate source of Canon Law is God, whose will is manifested through Divine Law. How can you and I argue against that? God is the highest authority there is, good Sister. I merely serve God's will, as do you. And with such a serious sin as this we must take care to follow the necessary actions."

"But murder is not just a sin, Your Eminence, it's a crime!" Sister Veronica's voice rose. "What about the body? Surely the police - "

"Am I not making myself clear, Sister?" Cardinal Moore spat, anger muddying his usual restraint. "Do you seek to argue with God? You, who have vowed to be obedient to him? There is no room for false prophets in the Roman Catholic Church, the one true church founded by Jesus, God's son. If you want to help then pray for this boy, commend him to the Lord. God's Laws, Divine Law and through him Canon Law, are the only ones acceptable to him. As a messenger of the Lord I can promise you this. Didn't Matthew say 'Beware of false prophets, which come to you in sheep's clothing'? I am sure you are not one of these, Sister. One who has promised to serve God but strays from him in times of great difficulty. Then your service to God and the Church would be meaningless, wouldn't it? No, listen to me, Sister. This murder has taken place on Church run property. Those who investigate Canon Law will deal with the body, I will personally supervise the matter. Does anyone else know of this?"

"No, not as far as I'm aware. I came to bake the students' cake, and discovered Jamie's body not ten minutes ago." Sister Veronica still shook, but now with a rage so pure she could hardly contain it.

"Thank you, Sister. I know I can rely on your absolute support and discretion in this matter. You need not say more about it just now, but in time I have no doubt that the Assessors will need to speak with you, while they gather the Acta, the documents that will become the basis of their investigation." Cardinal Moore spoke calmly now, but he moved closer. He's like a bird of prey bearing down on me, Sister Veronica thought. He's trying to silence me with his power. "I am responsible here, don't forget," the Cardinal continued, now very close to her. "I have overseen many other cases within the jurisdiction of Canonical Law and I will see that God's will is done here, with yours and Father Mathers help, of course."

Turning abruptly, he addressed the priest, who'd unfrozen and had been following the exchange of words keenly.

"Father Mathers. See that this matter is kept private at all costs. The students and anyone else wanting to enter the hostel must be kept away."

"Of course, Your Grace." Father Mathers replied. "You have my unending support, I will do everything I can to help you fulfil God's will in this and every matter. Where should the students go? All their belongings are in their rooms?"

"Find a solution. Do it discreetly and do not give a hint of any scandal. If journalists get hold of this story they will descend on us like rabid hyenas. Then all the good people of the cloth will yet again be attacked by inaccurate, deceiving, poisonous words. We are taught in seminary, are we not, Father Mathers, of the importance of close brotherhood, enacted for us through the apostolic tradition? Well now is the time for that brotherhood - and of course sisterhood - to come together. We must close ranks, and do justice for the boy. We must protect Mother Church, and we must bring whoever committed this monstrous sin to justice, in the most unobtrusive ways possible. In time we will have the *Res iudicata*, the final conclusion to this case. Until then, let us pray for the boy and his family, and for guidance, and let us all act in a unified manner according to God's will."

"Of course, Your Eminence. Sister Veronica and I will see this is done," Father Mathers said, his eyes flashing towards the nun for a second. A warning shot?

"Good. I must go now, there is much I have to organise with this. And to think we came here to speak of press coverage. So much can change within twenty minutes. I will take my leave of you good people. God Bless you both."

He turned and strode through the doorway back into the hostel, Father Mathers following like a lap dog.

Sister Veronica stared down at Jamie's body. I never promised anything, she thought. I was told what to do, but I never promised. My God would want me to help this boy, and that's what I'm going to do.

Chapter Five

Ascending the hostel stairs as quietly as she could manage, Sister Veronica heard the low murmured voices of Cardinal Moore and Father Mathers near the front door. Let them talk, she said to herself. Let the Cardinal warn Father Mathers to keep an eye on me, to make sure I behave. Knowing the clerics could not see the stairs from the front door, she trod on each stair as lightly as possible, her knees aching with the effort, willing each not to creak. She was glad they were talking. A few minutes grace would serve her nicely.

Through the window on the first floor landing, she caught a glimpse of a batch of bedraggled tourists faithfully following a tour guide down the street. The patch of wet grass at the centre of Soho Square was now empty, bar one dog walker. Strange how normal life goes on amid one's spiralling chaos, she thought. That must be what enables us to all keep going. Those in destruction and those in normality are carried along together, offset by each other, stuck together in this peculiar jigsaw we call life.

Now, which of these rooms was Jamie's? She'd kept to the ground floor before, never finding it necessary to impose on the personal spaces of hostel stayers, unless one had left and the room needed cleaning.

The first door she opened let out a pungent perfumed smell. Bottles of hair and beauty products were scattered across the desk, and the duvet was a soft pink colour, a French novel thrown on top of it. Probably that pretty girl Celine's room. She closed the door and tried more, but none of them seemed like Jamie's. He was fastidiously neat, she'd noticed, to a point of obsession, and none of the rooms had that feel about them. However, opening the second to last door along the corridor, and seeing the bare looking room, with its black duvet stretched meticulously over the bed, the three biros lined up with precision on the desk, and no other objects in sight anywhere else, suggested she may have found what she was looking for.

Entering the room, she imagined Jamie with her, staring at her in the intense way he'd had. Who were you? She asked him. What can you tell me that will let me help you?

Practical enough to feel no sense of guilt at going through a deceased person's belongings, Sister Veronica began searching the room. Opening the wardrobe doors exposed a rail of neatly hung shirts, mainly jeans and hooded tops, each hanger spaced evenly apart. She fingered through them, patting the pockets of the hoodies. The bottom of the cupboard was bare, apart from an empty sports bag. She drew back the plain blue curtains and looked behind. Only a spider. Going over to the desk, she pulled open the top drawer, revealing neatly rolled socks and underwear. The one beneath contained t-shirts folded and stacked to a mathematical degree, and the one beneath that, a vast selection of pills, as well as bottles of deodorant and shampoo. Sister Veronica picked up one of the pill packets and read, "Sertraline 200mg". What was that? Another said "Lithium Carbonate 1.5g". Puzzled by the extent of the boy's pharmaceutical stockpile, she closed the drawer and gazed at the biros on the desk. Now, if you have biros, you must have been writing something. But what?

Glancing round the room told her that the only other visible items were a pair of worn-looking black shoes. With great effort and wincing at the effect on her knees, she slowly crouched down and peered under the bed. Nothing. She lifted up the mattress, unsettling the perfectly folded sheet. Well, it wouldn't matter now. Jamie was somewhere else, and she prayed he was at peace. Nothing there either.

What an empty room. It was sad, she felt, that this amounted to the existence of the boy. No pictures or photos on the wall, no books or signs of any hobby. Where was his art? Wasn't he supposed to be an art student? She felt an uneasiness. Who on earth had Jamie Markham really been? She needed to approach the room differently. She hadn't been through enough. With renewed rigour she took initiative and reopened the middle drawer of the desk, lifting up the pile t-shirts, revealing a dog-eared plain black diary. Seizing it she flicked through the pages. Where was April? Ah yes. She flicked to the date, and stared. The only entry for that day said "Today's the day: Tell Sister Veronica". Jamie had drawn a smiley face in a perfect circle next to the words. Tell Sister Veronica what?

Footsteps on the stairs made her instinctively shove the diary under the duvet and close the door. She opened the wardrobe door and seized a handful of shirts, hangers slipping as she dragged them out.

"Sister Veronica! What on earth are you doing?" Father Mathers stood in the doorway, aghast.

"I'm following His Eminence's instructions, Father Mathers. The Cardinal clearly said that no students must be allowed back, so obviously they need to be housed elsewhere. If they can't be here, then we need to quickly clear their belongings out don't we? This room looked like it needed the least work, so I thought I'd start here. I'm quite surprised it's taken you this long to come and help, given the gravity of the situation. Not only do we need to do this, but we need to find somewhere else for the students to stay." She looked him squarely in the eye.

"Heaven's above, you wretched woman. What if this is Jamie's room? The Assessors won't want his possessions touched. That is the first thing we need to establish, which room was the boy's, and leave it just so. Honestly, no logic." Father Mathers shock must have completely left him as his pomposity was in full force. "I'll start at one end of the corridor and make my way up, you start at this end and we will establish which room is his; look for identifiable features, name tags, anything." He went off. Sister Veronica grabbed the notebook, it fitted into the deep pocket of her skirt. She hung the shirts back up, nowhere as neatly as Jamie had done, then went out of the room and loudly opened the end door very loudly, making a great show.

Before long Father Mathers had established that the room the nun had been messing about in was indeed Jamie's and he shook his head like a disappointed school teacher.

"Have you replaced the shirts, Sister? Exactly as you found them? Good. Then I think we don't need to mention your faux-pas to anyone. His Eminence is distraught enough as it is, and we don't want to make matters even worse. But learn from this and be more restrained in all other actions, please. Now let's get on with emptying the other rooms."

They were down to the last two rooms, packing the contents in large black bin bags Sister Veronica had found under the sink, when she heard cheery voices from outside, and a key turning in the lock.

"The students are back," Father Mathers called imperiously from the next door room. "I'll go down and explain something to them while you finish the rooms. Can't have you messing anything else up today, can we, Sister?"

She heard him go down the stairs and intercept the students at the door.

"We're terribly sorry," she could hear him explaining, "but unfortunately a severe carbon monoxide leak has been identified and the building has been deemed unsafe to live in for now. Yes, yes, Sister Veronica is packing up your belongings at the moment, but the authorities have told us that none of you are to be allowed back in, for your own safety. We are awfully sorry for the inconvenience, please accept this money and go to the café down the street. We are in the process of finding you alternative accommodation. Yes it will be free of charge, as you've already paid your hostel fees. One of us will come and get you when we know where that is."

"How easily lying comes to you, Father Mathers," Sister Veronica said under her breath, as she tied a knot in a bulging bag. "Almost as though you're practised at it." She was sure Cardinal Moore would be thrilled at being billed for accommodation for the students, but this secrecy was at his insisting, so he dashed well pay for the blasted collateral damage.

A new voice from outside made her stop her work and pause.

"What's going on here?" It was Father John's voice. "Is everything alright?"

Father Mathers lowered his voice so she couldn't hear his reply, but she was certain he wouldn't be divulging the truth. Oh no, he had his eye on bigger things in life, just as she was sure Cardinal Moore had his eye on Rome. Neither of them would compromise their ambitions, she would bet her entire stash of writings on it.

"We'll call you later then, Father John," Father Mathers said loudly, a few minutes later. "Let you know how the students are. Yes, yes, she's fine, please don't worry."

Well that's a pity, Sister Veronica sighed. She had an insatiable desire to talk to a friend, to someone who cared more about others than their own reputation and desires. Of course she couldn't tell them about the terrible things that had occurred today, but having contact with human compassion when times were tough was healing almost above all else, in her opinion. By Jove, she didn't know how she was going to handle this. Not just Jamie's murder, but the Cardinal's reaction to it. Surely it wasn't right? Surely the police needed to know?

 Later that evening, after the students had been split up and rehoused in three other hostels across London, the chaos of their belongings in bin bags finally sorted out and returned to the rightful owners, Cardinal Moore fully updated, the carbon monoxide cover story spread liberally throughout the convent, the keys of the next door hostel handed over to two men dressed all in black, no dog collars, who had strode up to the convent at twenty to six in the evening bringing a decidedly chilly air with them – presumably the Cardinal's Assessors although Sister Veronica couldn't possibly say as they'd hardly introduced themselves – she finally had a chance to sit down with a cup of tea and some toast. She'd brought them up to her room, not caring if this would be frowned on by Sister Irene. Starving, emotionally battered, angry, perplexed and overwhelmingly exhausted, all she wanted was to eat and drink, then lie down and have a proper read of Jamie's diary and try and find out what on earth he meant by "Tell Sister Veronica". There was a gentle tap tap tap at her door.

"What?" She roared, slamming the plate of toast onto her desk. "What is it?" If it was Sister Irene, with a basket of apples and a homily about toast crumbs, she could –

"Only me," Sister Agnes' gentle voice called. "It doesn't sound like a good time, Veronica, should I come back tomorrow?"

"No," Sister Veronica heaved herself up and opened the door. "No, sorry Agnes, come in. I've had such a day. I'm glad you're here actually, I need to ask you something."

She stood aside so that her friend, stooping slightly, could shuffle in. Her eyes glanced down at Sister Agnes' swollen, red knuckles, and her knobbly misshapen fingers that stuck out randomly like branches on an old tree.

"How's the pain?" She asked, supporting her friend's elbows as she lowered herself slowly onto the edge of Sister Veronica's bed.

"Oh you know, comes and goes," Sister Agnes had no time for self-indulgence, especially when it came to illness. Sister Veronica always remembered the time when Sister Agnes had told her about a particular incident from her childhood. Her parents had kept horses, who she claimed her mother had doted on much more than on her five children. One day, Agnes, her mother, and two of her brothers had been off on a hack, cantering over open fields near their house, when Agnes' horse had been startled by a tractor suddenly swinging into the field. It became skittish, jumping sideways, and Agnes fell off, landing hard on her backside and fracturing her coccyx. Her mother's only advice, seeing her daughter writhe in agony in the subsequent days, was to tell her to rub the affected area hard with a brick. Sister Veronica suspected that this played a key part in Sister Agnes' continuing dismissal of her own and anyone else's pain, but still, it affected her to see her friend's laboured movements and inflamed joints.

Sister Veronica saw her friend eyeing her carefully.

"Have you got any more writing for me to read yet?" Sister Agnes asked, resting her hands on her lap. "I could do with a distraction from this infernal heat."

"Nothing worth showing you I'm afraid." Sister Veronica turned her desk chair around and sat down. She attempted to slow her breaths, she needed to decelerate her panicking heart rate and for the revulsion in her head to subside. She didn't want to lie to her friend, but what choice did she have? "This week's been unusually busy, what with the girl Melissa's interview, and packing up the students' belongings today. I smelt like a perfume factory after bundling up Celine's room."

"Hmm. Strange business, this carbon monoxide leak," Sister Agnes' beady eyes glinted. While her body had its pains, her mind was the sharpest in the convent, in Sister Veronica's opinion, it didn't miss a trick. She badly wanted to tell her friend exactly what had happened today but she daren't. The horror, coursing through her veins the minute she'd found Jamie, had multiplied and gone off on tangents after the Cardinal's reaction. She'd felt the heavy weight of danger descend on her when the police were not allowed to be called, so apart from anything else she didn't want to involve her already vulnerable friend in this murkiness. But oh how she longed to confide in Agnes. "Especially after the health and safety chap signed the hostel devices off as safe not more than a month ago. Sister Irene was beside herself with the fact we didn't need to spend any money buying new ones."

Sister Veronica's smile was ghostly-weak.

"All I can say is that's what the students were told," she said. "And another thing I can say, Agnes, is that I need to ask your advice about something. Now, this is going to sound strange but I'm going to have to ask you to trust me, and not to ask me any details, because I simply can't say at the moment. I have no doubt it will all come out in the end, but for now please don't press me on this." She looked at her friend, who stared back, then nodded. "You and your clever mind have been following the reports into the clerical sexual abuse disgraces, haven't you? I know you've been interested in the legalities?"

"I've certainly read about them in the papers," Sister Agnes replied. One aspect connected to her rheumatism that she didn't object to, was being allowed to read and rest in the library down the road several times a week. Her gnarled hands made it impossible for her to help with most of the nuns chores like cooking, cleaning and gardening, so a few years ago Mother Superior had suggested Sister Agnes might like to try the library as a diversion to keep her occupied, a proposition that had been readily agreed with. "It's all smoke and mirrors". The two nuns had established a long time ago that they both felt out of sorts with the management and power within the Catholic Church. It wasn't something they spoke of often, one had to be so careful, but it was comforting to know a shared view existed.

"Alright, so tell me this. Is Canonical Law really put above civil law in cases where sins or crimes have been committed within the church's remit?"

Sister Agnes raised her eyebrows.

"Yes," she said. "This has happened in many cases. In 2009 The Murphy report showed that in Ireland, bishops and archbishops had been supplied with multiple batches of conclusive evidence about priests who'd abused children, but dealt with this internally and never told the police. When the judge questioned them about this in court, they defended their decisions, despite suicides of the young victims in question being brought to the fore. They talked about how in civil law, defamation can only be committed through false statements, but how in church law defamation involves both the sin of calumny *and* the sin of detraction. Detraction is the unjust damaging of another's good name by the revelation of some fault or crime of which that other is in fact guilty, or at any rate is seriously believed to be guilty by the defamer."

Sister Veronica's stomach heaved.

"Are you saying," she said. "That under church law, even if someone is guilty, it is against the law to accuse them as guilty of the sin or crime committed, because you would be damaging their reputation?"

"Yes, that's exactly what I'm saying," Sister Agnes replied. "Evidence in The Murphy report states it clearly. I remember it so well because it repelled me to read it."

Sister Veronica banged her fist down hard on her desk. Tears flowed from her eyes.

"What exactly is this institution we're part of, Agnes?" She asked, her mind a pool of darkness. "This duplicity and dishonesty makes me sick to my soul. It makes a mockery of St Paul's belief in love as greater than all things. I'm no fool, I've been aware of the more corrupt sides of the church for some time now. I mean, how can one not be? But this? This is too much. I can no longer be involved with the tenets of this organisation. Where is God in the church nowadays? Why have men's egos overtaken basic truth? And love? Clearly no longer necessary. Oh, the hypocrisy." Her fist thumped down on the desk again. She experienced a deep shudder of knowing as the sheer enormity of the murder, the secrecy, her involvement, and Cardinal Moore's immediate instinct to put the welfare of the church's reputation over and above justice for Jamie sunk in.

Sister Agnes let her friend's sobs subside until they sat quietly together, solitude calming the pain. Then she leaned forward.

"Now, listen here, Veronica. No, look at me, and listen to what I've got to say. I don't know what went on in the hostel today, and I'm not going to ask. But what I do know is that you shouldn't give up, not now. Don't you dare. My body's too broken for me to be of any use, but you still have your health, and you have the passion to bring some light into whatever darkness you're seeing. I agree with you, there's a stench of corruption that runs deeply in this institution, and I hate it. Oh, there's plenty of good people, but so many are being misled by those drunk with power. I can't do anything about it, but you can. We've made our beds here, but we don't have to lie in them. Can't you see that? You can do something, anything, that will help. Whatever it is that's happened, if it's being covered up, you don't have to be one of those who sits mildly by and does nothing. I don't think you would ever do that anyway," Sister Agnes finished, with a wry smile. "You're too bloody minded".

Sister Veronica gazed at her friend. She breathed several times very deeply. She thought about Jamie's words, how he was going to tell her something. Was it more than a coincidence that he was murdered on the same day that he planned to reveal information to her? Damn it all. A small part of her wanted to ignore all this, until it went away. But a larger, lioness part of her reared up in anger and protection towards Jamie.

"Looks like I won't have much time for writing in the near future then, doesn't it?" She said.

Opening her bedroom door to see her friend off, the sight of the fire door at the end of the corridor closing made her start. Had someone been listening to their conversation? No, stop it, Veronica. It's probably one of the Sisters going off to have a bath. She would not give in to the clawing hands of paranoia, no matter how hard they tried to get her in their grasp.

Chapter Six

Melissa Carlton lay on her narrow bed, strands of golden and pink hair splayed across the pillow. A new nicotine patch slapped on the inside of her arm, she breathed out with relief as the irritation induced by withdrawal receded.

She had vague plans to give up smoking, but that certainly wasn't top of her priority list right now. Bloody hell, she couldn't keep this up for long, or she'd be a wreck. She was wondering what the actual fuck had happened to her life. One minute she'd been a party-loving hard working, hard living journalist, the next minute she was holed up in a convent without her phone, on an insane one person mission that at best felt surreal, and at worst rash, badly planned and disastrous. And all for this bloody secret that had been shoved on her, that she didn't want.

She didn't believe in fate but some events were too synchronistic to go unnoticed. The internal workings of this convent were complex, it didn't take a genius to see that. On the surface, the Sisters, and the priests when they came, had given up their free will, and their official line was that they all had callings to serve God. As far as she could tell, Sister Irene was the only old girl who believed what she said one hundred percent. But things were not as straightforward as they seemed. Some people's individuality wasn't squashed yet; in particular, Sister Veronica's eyes spoke louder than words.

When the co-ordinator of the secret French support group, the one that helped all the other people round the world who'd been born into the same secret, unwanted club she'd been, had given her the name Jamie Markham: "He's in Westminster too, try and find him", it hadn't taken her long to find out that he worked in the hostel next door. She blinked with frustration. Why had she left it so long to talk to him? What if it was too late now? From what she'd seen and heard over the last day she wondered if she'd ever get a chance now. For God's sake, she was an idiot to get into all this in the first place.

Her mission – for what? Answers? Recognition? Peace? – had taken an unexpected left hand turn yesterday. It was beyond strange and worrying. What she'd witnessed outside the hostel, after asking Mother Superior if she could pop to the chemist on the pretext of getting necessary "ladies products", kept playing in her mind. She recalled the scene intensely, raking it over, trying to make sense of the details. How come she'd left the convent, desperate for some new nicotine patches, and been present at the exact moment it happened? There was one woman who could help her, but she felt with all her intuition that she was the last person

Sister Veronica would want to talk to at the moment. But there was no way in hell she was going to give up, she was just going to have to make the old nun listen. Of course, she'd have to confess to her that she hadn't just come to the convent to investigate and write a piece on "How Nun's Live", although she was doing that too, her editor had loved the idea when she'd pitched it. Her journalistic purpose justified her presence, and diverted attention away from her real motive. No one had looked at her strangely so far, apart from Sister Veronica. And she looked at everyone like they were half baked. She'd almost given herself away when she'd interviewed the old girl in the garden; let her guard down for a moment, and Sister Veronica had clocked that something was up. But there was no way she could have known what it was. She hoped she'd be able to win Sister Veronica's confidence, but she had a hit and miss history with that kind of thing. How had Darren her dickhead ex, ceremoniously dumped last Friday, described her? "You're fucking crazy," he'd hissed as she'd walked away from him. "And your heart is stone. You're going to die lonely, and that's just what you deserve." This wasn't true, her heart was most definitely not made from stone. In truth she'd always had too many emotions to deal with but she found a hard shell a good defence against the world, and Darren. He'd changed from attentive to critical over the two years they'd spent together, so there'd been no other option, he'd had to go. One thing Melissa was good at doing was walking away from a problem. Would she walk away from this too?

She already knew the answer. No, she wouldn't – couldn't – walk away from this one. She was no shrink, but she did sometimes worry that she was crazy, she had such a fluid sense of identity, she didn't feel like she knew who she was at all, and she highly suspected this was because of her parental situation; biological and adoptive. It was so bloody cliché it was unbelievable. Her anxiety, that she usually managed to hide in the daytime, had been in overdrive at night; racing thoughts, a floating sense of being outside her body, it all felt out of control. It was scary and she wanted it to stop. She looked younger than her twenty nine years – everybody said so. But inside her the ubiquitous clock was ticking, and she wanted to meet someone, maybe even have a kid, before she was in danger of becoming one of those mums in the playground that everyone thought was a granny. But that wasn't likely to happen until she got to the root of the problem. She was doing this for herself, Melissa knew. She was finally going to sort herself out.

Minutes later, nicotine patch hidden under a long, flowing shirt, she rapped at Sister Veronica's door. A low grumbling could be heard, then the door opened.

"I hope I'm not disturbing you?" Melissa smiled brightly.

The look of sheer resignation and dismay on the nun's face answered her question.

"I'm sorry, Melissa, but I'm a bit busy at the moment" Sister Veronica said gruffly, closing the door. Melissa's foot arrived swiftly as a doorstop.

"With respect, Sister Veronica," Melissa said, her voice lower. "I need to talk to you. Sorry to sound dramatic, but I'm not leaving your room until I have."

"Melissa!" The nun was instantly angry. "Have you forgotten yourself?"

Melissa sighed. She was going to have to bring the big guns out.

"It's about Jamie Markham," she whispered.

Sister Veronica glared.

"You'd better come in," she said.

The nun's bedroom wasn't the sparse space Melissa had been expecting. It was a place of business; a wodge of papers and notebooks was piled high on the desk with an old black notebook on top, pens strewn around, an empty plate at one end. The bed was roughly made, the crumpled duvet suggested Sister Veronica had been lying on top of it recently. A skirt was thrown over the back of the desk chair, and a stash of books piled up in one corner of the room.

Sister Veronica turned the desk chair around roughly, motioned for Melissa to sit down, then sat on the bed.

"Well?" she said.

"Look, I don't really know where to start." Melissa glanced at the door, checking it was shut. "I haven't been completely honest with you, Sister. I'm here for more reasons than just research."

Sister Veronica continued her glare.

Melissa took a deep breath.

"I've known for three years now that my birth mother is a nun. I was brought up knowing I was adopted, but with no information about who my biological parents were. On her deathbed, my aunt told me the truth, she said I had a right to know. She said my birth mother was a nun from the Diocese of Westminster, but that my adoptive parents didn't want me to know. They are very Catholic, they want to protect the church. My mum was furious with my aunt, she won't tell me my birth mother's name, and my aunt didn't know. There's a support group for the children of clergy in France, I found it on the internet. I started Googling biological children of nuns the minute I found out, I wanted to speak to someone in the same situation, I felt so isolated, you can't imagine. Then one day this group popped up. I got in touch with them, and they've really helped me. They put me in touch with other nuns and priests' children, it turns out there's loads of us, but we've all been kept secrets. When I told the guy from the support group that I was a journalist, he suggested I find a way to gain access to the Diocese of Westminster, he says you get so much more knowledge when you work with the Catholic Church rather than against it. I'd tried everything else to find my birth mother and failed, so I thought I'd give it a go. I didn't mean any harm, Sister, honestly. I just want to find my biological mother so badly. You don't know what it's like, not knowing who your real parents are."

The old nun continued staring at her, unblinking.

"Just before I arrived at The Convent of the Christian Heart, the group's co-ordinator sent me a message. He said he'd heard another child of clergy was about in Westminster, the child of a priest, called Jamie Markham. He said I should try and find him, and that maybe we could help each other."

With this information, Sister Veronica's eyes filled with pain and tears, and she sagged as though hit by an unseen weapon, but still she sat, staring at Melissa.

"A couple of days ago, I found out that Jamie worked at the hostel next door. I overheard Sister Irene telling Sister Maria what an un-talkative boy he was. I was planning to go and speak to him, but I wanted to interview the Sisters first. I didn't know how Jamie would react when I spoke to him, and if he blew my cover I wouldn't be able to stay here anymore." Melissa sighed. "Then yesterday, after I asked Mother Superior if I could pop to the shops to get something I badly needed, I saw some men dressed in black going into the youth hostel. It was after the whole drama with the carbon monoxide leak. They didn't look like technicians, one had a gold cross round his neck. The other was wheeling a big suitcase through the hostel door. It just seemed really strange."

The pain and hurt in Sister Veronica's eyes intensified.

"I really regretted not talking to Jamie while I had the chance, and now that the students have been re-housed all over London I thought I better get in touch with him before I lost the opportunity forever. So this morning I told Sister Julia I had a meeting I'd forgotten about with my editor, and that I really must go to it. She wasn't pleased, but she agreed. I know this was a little bit of an untruth, Sister, but I really had to find Jamie."

Sister Veronica responded to this information with an unflinching agony-filled gaze.

"So then," Melissa went on. "I went to all the hostels Sister Catherine said the students had been re-homed in, looking for him. But he wasn't in any of them, and the students said they hadn't seen him since yesterday morning at breakfast. One of them gave me his mobile number, and I tried to ring it from a pay phone – Mother Superior said she wouldn't give me my phone back till the end of the week – but it just went to voicemail. I know this sounds strange, Sister, but I'm really worried about him. Do you know where he is?"

Sister Veronica considered this question.

"It seems to me," she said heavily. "That so much has been going on right under my nose, and that I've missed it all."

Chapter Seven

Sister Veronica's head was reeling. Jamie, the child of a priest? Was that what he was going to tell her yesterday? Was this why someone had killed him, to silence him?

The parallels between Jamie and Melissa's stories and her own life were too excruciating to contemplate, yet they couldn't be ignored. And she had thought she was the only one. She'd found out that day, when she was thirteen, when she'd gone into the church with a message from her mum for the priest about the flowers. A reptilian chill permeated her skin as she remembered how she'd gone into the church, calling Father Dominic's name, eventually finding the priest in the vestry.

He'd been hoping she'd pop in, he said. Her mother had said she might. Yes, yes, a new flower arrangement on Saturday afternoon would be just the thing. She hadn't immediately understood the predatory hunger in the priest's eyes. But when he'd pushed her against the wall and done unspeakable things to her, she'd understood. Good girl, he'd said. You've made me do this. Look at the dress you wore. This is our little secret. Even now, as the flashback tormented her, she could smell that awful mustiness laced with incense and candle wax, feel his body against hers. Afterwards, with hot tears falling down her cheeks formed from terror and disgust, she'd whispered,

"You're a bad man. I'm going to tell my father."

"Your father?" The priest had laughed. "You silly girl, has no one told you? He's no father of yours. You are just like your mother now, a dirty whore. No one will believe you, least of all that poor cuckolded man. Your real father's been moved on now. Why do you think Father Simon left the parish all those years ago?"

Weeks later, when she could speak again, she'd asked her mother.

"Was my real daddy Father Simon?"

Her mother had wept. Shhh, she'd said. Who told you? Don't ever mention this again. I was wrong, Veronica, I did a bad thing. But I atone for my sins every day. We must protect the church's good name, Veronica. Don't mention this, even to your father. It hurts him too much. Just forget you ever found out, put it out of your mind, do you hear? I never want to hear another word about this.

But things had never been the same again. She – Veronica - had atoned too, every day, for her parents' sins, for the priest's sin, and for her sin. Until one day, as she stood on top of a waterfall near their farm, looking down, down, down at the water crashing on the rocks below. I could be crashing on the rocks too – the thought sped through her mind in a second. And the pain would be over. Then she realised. This is their guilt. I can't carry it anymore. In a split second she'd felt free. Not completely free, just as though a certain weight had disappeared. What had remained was an incandescent anger, a seething spark of rage at the baseless lack of humanity in some people that caused them to hurt others. And when that lack of humanity came from people of the cloth, priests and nuns, her rage became unending. With the new knowledge Melissa had brought today, Jamie's fight had instantly become her own. Their suffering was the same, but Jamie was dead, killed – it seemed – to cover another's mistake.

Now, she stared at the girl in front of her. If everything Melissa said could be trusted, there was a very real chance that the girl could now also be in danger. She stared at the girl, and her instinct told her that Melissa was telling the truth. Oh, how she wished none of this had happened, how she longed for her previous life of just two days ago. But it *had* happened, and for some reason God and the universe had chosen to make her a key cog in its wheel. A strange calmness came over her. She would do what needed to be done, no matter what the consequences. And God protect anyone who got in her way. She frowned.

"Melissa," she said slowly. "I am about to tell you something that you must promise not to tell anyone, ANYONE, for your own sake?"

The girl nodded.

"Jamie is dead," Sister Veronica said. "And from what you've told me, I have reason to believe your life might be in danger too."

"What do you mean, dead?" Shock rendered Melissa's face ghostly white. "How do you know?"

Sister Veronica got up, opened her bedroom door, and looked both ways down the corridor. Then she closed the door, sat back down on her bed, and told Melissa about yesterday's events. About going over to the hostel with the ingredients, finding Jamie's body, the visit from the Cardinal and Father Mathers, and Cardinal Moore's decision to keep the matter within Canonical Law.

"But he can't do that," Melissa's protest was loud. "It's illegal. What about Jamie's parents and family?"

"They'll be paid off, I expect," Sister Veroncia said darkly. "Silence money, whether they want it or not. Sometimes confidentiality agreements are forced on people, and they're legally binding. I went to the library early this morning to read how church law has handled clerical sexual abuse cases, I wanted to understand the precedents for Cardinal Moore's actions. Often large sums of money have been swapped for the family's silence, and I'll bet that's what will happen here."

Melissa's body folded until it was bent double in the chair, her hands took hold of large clumps of her hair and gripped until her knuckles became taut and white. When her sobs started, they were violent and noisy, a primal reaction to a universal horror. Sister Veronica stood up and placed her hand on Melissa's back, waiting for the inevitable onslaught to pass.

While she waited, a series of questions pressed forward in her mind and clamoured for attention. Why had Jamie been killed? Was it an inside job or a burglary gone wrong? Perhaps Jamie had been involved with the wrong sort of people; he had enough pills to open a pharmacy. Who was Jamie's father? Was the father involved, was he killed to stop Jamie telling anyone of his connection with the ordained? Something that had been troubling her since yesterday pressed forward too. Was the Cardinal really within his rights not to report this matter to the police?

Saints alive, how on earth was she going to set about answering even one of these questions? Reading Jamie's diary last night hadn't told her much, the entries were very short and perfunctory: "Arrived in Soho", "Talked to Dominique", "Spoke to Victor, have agreed to do it". Who were Dominique and Victor? Certainly none of the hostel students went by those names. What had he agreed to do? The questions were mounting but so far she could answer none of them.

Thoughts of her murder-mystery manuscript flashed through her mind. In the seven crime stories she'd completed so far, she always made her detective character, DI Nancarrow, follow a process when he investigated murders. He assessed the crime scene, spoke to witnesses, collected evidence and interviewed suspects. She made she he wrote down everything, creating a timeline of events, and he had to follow every lead. He looked for what instigated the murder, the motivation behind it. Fine, this was fiction and what she was dealing with was real life. But it was all the structure she had, so it just might help. She'd have to go back to the hostel and take another look, for starters.

After several minutes, the girl's sobs quietened.

"This is too horrible," Melissa's voice was muffled. "I can't believe this is happening. I can't handle this. If I'd gone to talk Jamie earlier, maybe I could have helped him. Maybe this wouldn't have happened."

"Maybe it would, maybe it wouldn't," Sister Veronica felt ruthless, but she had to get through to the girl. "Maybe if I'd gone over earlier, or taken more time to get to know the boy, it wouldn't have happened either. But neither of us killed Jamie. That was someone else, maybe more than one person. The guilt lies with them, not us, and it won't bring him back to torment ourselves with blame."

Melissa managed a watery smile.

"You're as sharp as a knife, aren't you Sister? I thought you were different from the rest of them."

"Oh, and why's that?" Sister Veronica couldn't help herself.

"It's the way you look at people, like you're constantly observing. Your eyes seem to take in everything."

It was Sister Veronica's turn to manage a thin smile.

"I do love people watching," she said. "I always have. It's how I make sense of the world."

She gazed at the shocked girl.

"What we need," she said, getting up and bustling about. "Is a bit of normality for a minute or two. And there's nothing more real than a packet of Custard Cream biscuits."

A few minutes later, they both sat with a pile of biscuits in their hands, Melissa nibbling hers and Sister Veronica working quickly through her batch with remarkable application.

"I never really liked these," Melissa said. "But at the moment they don't taste too bad."

"Best thing ever invented, in my opinion," Sister Veronica said stoutly, reaching again for the packet.

The peak of the shockwave had broken, and the crisis – while still in full swing – was at least laid out bare for them both to see. Melissa rubbed the side of her head.

"Hang on," she said. "What did you mean when you said you think my life might be in danger too?"

"My dear," Sister Veronica shook her head. "There's more I need to tell you. Yesterday, as the Cardinal was leaving, I went upstairs to look in Jamie's room. I feel as strongly as you do that the powers that be are not handling this case in an ethical or moral way. They are protecting themselves, their reputations, and the public image of the church. They don't seem to care about getting justice for Jamie, they just want it all cleaned up as quickly and as quietly as possible. You said before that I couldn't know what it's like to not know your parentage, or the desire to find your roots. I'm afraid you're wrong there, Melissa, I know that feeling very well. This seems an unbelievable thing for me to admit to you, because no one else in this convent knows, but when I was thirteen, I was told that my real father was the local priest, Father Simon. He was transferred to another parish soon after my mother gave birth, and the matter was never spoken of again. I always thought I was the only priest's child in existence until you told me about yourself and Jamie, and this group. I am now no longer alone in this, it's a wonderful and terrifying feeling. Although I'm finding it hard to comprehend the numbers of priests' and nuns' children in existence that you seem to be implying."

"I know, I know exactly how you feel," Melissa said. "I couldn't believe it either. But you have to believe me, Sister Veronica. I can show you the group, I can introduce you to some of the others. There are loads of us. Honestly, it's the best kept secret since they discovered the world was round." Melissa's eyes bored into hers imploringly. "If you think about it, it kind of makes sense. Priests and nuns are human too. Taking a vow of celibacy one day might seem a good idea, but forever is a long time. This was going to be the subject of my next article, after the one about this convent. I've already started making notes for it. Cardinal Wolsey, in Henry VIII's time, confessed to having at least two kids. Erasmus was the son of a Catholic priest. You can see on Wikipedia that lots of Popes have admitted to fathering loads of kids. We've always been out there, we've just never known about each other before. The internet is a wonderful thing."

"It sometimes is, it sometimes isn't, from what I hear," Sister Veronica said. "I've never really used it."

They sat quietly for a minute.

"It might be safer for you to return home, Melissa," Sister Veronica said gently. Seeing the girl distraught, and learning of their shared experiences had softened her feelings considerably. "We could make up a story, say you're feeling sick and need to go?"

Melissa grimaced.

"Go where? Home to my empty apartment, knowing everything that I do, and just resume normal life as though I don't have a care in the bloody world? Yeah, that's such a realistic option." Her face dropped into a cold, detached look.

"I can't allow anything else to happen here, not now I know all that I do. I'm trying to think about your safety, Melissa, can't you see that?" It came out more sharply than Sister Veronica had intended. "A boy has been killed, do you understand? This is a dangerous place, and while you're here, you could be a sitting target. And I will not allow that, not on my watch. The best thing is for you to return home immediately."

"Of course I understand," Melissa said, standing up. "I'm scared shitless, Sister, if I'm honest. But I don't see how sending me home is going to make me any safer. If it's as dangerous around here as you say, and people have been watching our movements, then going home by myself makes me a sitting duck. I might as well write "Home alone, come and kill me" on my front door. If anyone wants to get me I'll be playing right into their hands. And I've got nowhere else to go." Fresh hot tears spilled from her eyes as she marched out of the room, shutting the door loudly behind her.

Chapter Eight

Feeling dispiritedly idle, Father Mathers poured himself another sweet sherry. That inconsequential little nun, Sister Veronica, was a pain in his side. It was her fault he'd started drinking before lunchtime again, and to think, he'd nearly managed to get out of that habit. She was like a terrier, always snapping at his heels, sniffing him out at the least convenient times. Why couldn't the woman learn her place? The Sisters were volunteers, there to serve, and should only offer their opinion when called on. This was the natural order of things, it was Divine Law, it was what God had decreed when he made only men apostles. He was going to have to break the old dog's strong-mindedness somehow.

Honestly, the woman was odious, far too smart. Her opinions were coarse, her comments too direct. She had no understanding of social nuances, it was uncouth and embarrassing. And to think that he, Zachary Mathers, who had risen to the rank of diocesan priest exceptionally quickly and now considered Cardinal Moore – the prince of the Catholic Church in Britain - a personal friend, should have to put up with this kind of behaviour from a female. It was distasteful; it maligned his sense of worth.

He was sure she'd overheard him talking in the convent the other day. Nosy old crow. He hadn't been doing anything wrong, and his business was none of hers anyway. Then of course she was there to upset His Eminence when the wretched boy's body was discovered yesterday. It was a damn shame, or course, the whole affair. But his Grace was right, it had to be dealt with internally, there was no question of that. He completely understood why the Cardinal had bestowed on him the responsibility of making sure she kept that bleating mouth of hers firmly shut. What he needed to do was to give the woman a bloody good fright. Take her down a step or two. Didn't the Early Church Fathers identify women as the cause evil entering the world? That race were lucky they'd been given a place in the Roman Catholic Church at all. As his wise old mother had always said, women should ultimately always defer to men. And she always knew best, God rest her soul.

He sipped his sherry and leaned back in his antique chair - taking care not to disturb his carefully parted hair - trying to shut irritating images of the old busy body out of his mind. His sleek black cat, Tertullian, eyed him lazily from the chaise longue on the other side of the room. After all, Father Mathers consoled himself, he'd already become accustomed to mixing within far higher circles. Soon, if all went to plan, he wouldn't have to see much of those tweed skirted Sisters down the street at all. Anxieties flooded his mind as he went through the logistics of what he needed to do. He, Father Zachary St John Mathers, a distinguished scholar and devout religious minister, deserved more in life and he was bloody well going to make sure he got it.

The telephone rang. Father Mathers rose gracefully from his chair.

"Hello, Father Mathers speaking?"

"I'm getting worried," a familiar voice said. "You're running out of time, and nothing's happening. I'm worried you're going to break the deal."

"I'm not going back on the deal," Father Mathers shouted. The fingers of his left hand went immediately to his temple. "I've told you before, I just need more time."

He slammed the phone down.

It rang again.

"Listen, will you just -"

"Ah, good afternoon, Bishop Hammett here." Father Mathers' blood pressure decreased. Ah, the Cardinal's secretary. After all they were all working together now, weren't they? "His Eminence has requested your presence at the Archbishop's House soon as possible, and asks if you could be on your way this very minute, with haste?"

"Of course, please tell His Grace I'll leave now," Father Mathers said.

"Excellent. God bless."

"God bless you Father."

Father Mathers gave a small smile as he put the phone down and treated himself to one last glass of light brown liquid. An idea had just occurred to him that – if put into play - would certainly hamper Sister Veronica's nose for interference. He had a feeling he might share it with Cardinal Moore that very afternoon. That other bastard could wait. With renewed vigour, he swallowed, placed the empty glass down and reached for his briefcase.

Chapter Nine

It was with relief that Sister Veronica sat down to lunch; leek and potato soup and a wholemeal roll, prepared today by Sister Maria. By Godfathers, she needed some sustenance and a minute or two of inconsequential chit chat with the other Sisters. Emotionally battered and bruised, she now had a resolute purposefulness goading her to look deeper into Jamie's death, and hang the consequences. If she could do this one useful thing with her life, even if it got her in to trouble, then so be it; her existence would mean something in the end. But this moment of reprieve was gratefully received, a fleeting experience of familiarity before she descended into the turmoil of murder again. Even Sister Irene's expounding of her delight at the Vatican's most recently made Saint – anything Sister Irene said usually had the effect of a cheese grater on her nerves - was strangely comforting.

Melissa was not at lunch, she noticed, but Sister Veronica had not expected her to be. She'd handled the situation badly, she knew that, she'd said the wrong thing to the girl, silly woman. She'd been too overbearing when what the girl needed was understanding and a patient ear. But how did one handle trauma in the right way? No excuses, Veronica. Eat your food then go and see Melissa and apologise.

Sister Mary was nodding along to Sister Irene's words.

"Papal supremacy is at the heart of my life," Sister Mary joined in, tearing her roll in half. "The Pope has spoken and I will follow him."

"God give us all the grace and humility to honour His Holiness," Sister Irene put her spoon down and bowed her head. "We are but sheep in his flock, and we must listen to our shepherd."

Sister Catherine chuckled.

"He's a very wealthy shepherd," she said. "I caught a headline on my way back from the soup kitchen yesterday. It said 'Vatican's Wealth Runs to Billions'".

"Sister!" Sister Irene's head snapped up. "As you well know, the Vatican's wealth is not disposable, these reports are mythical. Our dear Church runs more hospitals and charity than any other religion in the world with its investments. I highly recommend you read the Catholic social doctrine before making light of His Holiness's resources."

"Alright, calm down Sister, my vocation is to serve the Pope too," Sister Catherine grinned. "Doesn't mean I can't mention the odd headline, does it Veronica?"

Sister Veronica grunted. She had no intention of being drawn into any lunchtime politics today.

"Where's Sister Anastasia?" Sister Maria's girlish voice spoke out. "Is she still unwell?"

"Sister Anastasia was taken to hospital last night," Sister Julia, the Mother Superior, dragged herself from her melancholic reverie to speak. "As most of you are aware, she was taken ill in the garden on the day of the carbon monoxide leak. She's been unable to speak since then, and last night her condition deteriorated. We will devote our afternoon prayers to her of course."

Sister Veronica sat up, surprised. Why hadn't she noticed poor Sister Anastasia was sick? Well, so much had happened, but still. She couldn't let her ties to her community slip. She was fond of Sister Anastasia, who'd always brought a grounding archaic air to the convent.

The rest of the meal passed in a staid unobtrusiveness, Sister Irene limiting herself to only occasional disapproving glances at Sister Catherine.

Sister Agnes gave her the odd encouraging grin from the opposite side of the table, which she returned each time, grimacing as best she could.

Father Adams, lap dog to Father Mathers, was sitting at table too, hardly able to eat anything, which Sister Veronica supposed was due to nerves as it was his first time leading prayers at the convent that afternoon. His golden hair glittered in the sun's rays that shot through the kitchen window. When he asked Sister Maria to please pass the butter, her cheeks flushed scarlet. Good Lord, Sister Veronica said to herself. The man's unstoppable.

Just as she was wiping her mouth and intending to stand up to help the rest of the Sisters clear the table, Sister Julia slapped her hand down on it hard.

"A storm is coming," the Mother Superior announced prophetically, "I can feel it."

Oh for heaven's sake, Sister Veronica muttered to herself, piling her soup bowl on top of others. She's so dramatic. You only have to look out of the window to see the clouds.

As she trudged up the flight of stairs towards Melissa's room, a plan of action formed in her mind. Perhaps she would share it with the girl, she wondered to herself. See what she thought? Maybe it would bond them together. Saints preserve her, she needed all the honest allies she could get at the moment. Up until now, she'd been approaching the whole debacle from the wrong angle, she'd realised. But now she knew what to do.

Puffing, as she arrived outside Melissa's door, Sister Veronica knocked three times. No answer.

"Hello?" She called. "Melissa, can I come in? I'm awfully sorry about before."

Still no answer.

A feeling of dread coursed through her. Suddenly expecting the worst, a flashback of Jamie's body in her mind, Sister Veronica threw the door open.

The room was empty, bare. The girl had gone. No personal possessions or the merest hint of Melissa left behind at all.

Entering the room, Sister Veronica picked up the piece of paper on the bed.

"Dear Mother Superior," she read. "Thank you so much for letting me stay in your convent, I have hugely enjoyed my time here. Unfortunately I had a bad asthma attack this morning, and my Ventolin is running low, so I need to go and get this sorted out. Apologies for my sudden departure, but I hope you understand. I've done enough research here for the article, which I promise will portray the Sisters in a positive light. I've taken my phone from the desk drawer in the office – please don't be cross. Thanks again and warmest regards to you all, Melissa."

Damn, dash and blast, and double drat.

Chapter Ten

Cardinal Moore rested both elbows on his desk and leaned forward. In front of him, sat two gentlemen, their countenances mild, both dressed conservatively. Sister Bernadette - reassigned from The Convent of the Christian Heart to the Archbishop's House six years ago due to her utterly discretionary nature - had just served them tea. Now they were alone, the door shut. An observer would have had no hint of any interrogatory undertones to the meeting, it was a civilised assembly between Men of God.

"I wanted to take this opportunity to ask how the investigation is going?" Cardinal Moore said.

"Very well, Your Eminence," one of the men replied. His suit was cut by the best tailor in Savile Row.

"Wonderful. May I conclude that no trace of evidence was left at the scene?" Cardinal Moore's calculating mind was exposed. He wanted to guard against any future unsavoury surprises.

"Nothing at all. We collected all the evidence, and have disposed of it in the usual way. The builders at the hostel have been reinstated, paid more for their quick return. They are pouring rubble into the back garden as we speak," the other man replied, his tone flat and professional.

"Perfect."

They all sipped their tea.

"The second stage of the plan begins immediately," Cardinal Moore spoke. "As before, there can be no mistakes."

"There won't be."

"Is the team assembled?"

"Of course, already in place, and under our surveillance."

"Very good." Cardinal Moore betrayed no hint of emotion. He rarely did. "How did the family take it?"

"They complied."

"Good. Remember, all humans have limitations. Make sure no one's emotional frailties hamper the operation at any stage."

"Of course, Your Grace. We are efficient at what we do."

"I know you are," the Cardinal murmured. He had worked with these men before. But warnings never went amiss, even with consummate professionals. It kept them on their toes. So he continued: "However - just to clarify - if events did go wrong, alternative, ah, interventions would be swiftly made."

The men nodded. They knew what this meant.

The man on the left retrieved a plain folder from his briefcase, and slid it across the table.

"Your paperwork, Your Eminence."

"Excellent," the Cardinal smiled faintly, appearing far younger than his sixty six years. He flicked open the folder's cardboard flap and saw a ticket for a return flight to Rome. He glanced at his watch. That man Mathers should be arriving any minute. He allowed his smile to stretch wider. Life was most definitely like a board game, he felt. Chess would be the closest analogy. And Mathers had an unequivocal pawness about him. A useful pawn, but still a pawn. The Cardinal closed the meeting with swiftness and expertise.

Chapter Eleven

So much thought, Father Mathers looked around the elegant interior Sister Bernadette had left him waiting in, had gone into this room. The furniture, the wallpaper, the lighting, it was all so magnificent, so tasteful; so understated yet opulent. He licked his lips. One day, perhaps he might - He chuckled. Don't get ahead of yourself, old boy. One step at a time.

He'd hugely enjoyed strutting into the Archbishop's House, past that downtrodden wretch Sister Cecelia who was mopping the floor, past Fathers Adebayo and Wade who were sitting behind the reception desk, and past the Cardinal's most trusted friend and his chief of staff and strategy, Bishop Sabell, who'd stared at him in the most unfriendly way. He hadn't cared a jot about how anyone looked at him. He, Father Mathers, was on the way up and no mistake.

While he waited, he adopted different sitting positions on the sofa, wondering which made him appear the most authoritative yet at the same time humbly servile and ingratiating. He was just in the middle of a position change when the door opened.

"Ah, Father Mathers," the Cardinal had put on his robes especially. He understood Mathers' admiration of status and possessions perfectly. "So good of you to come."

"Of course, Your Grace. I would do anything for you."

"That really is the most marvellous news," Cardinal Moore smiled as he sat down. "Stuffy weather today?"

"Yes, at least we've had no more rain. The forecast says thunderstorms later."

"Oh dear, how trying," the Cardinal said. "Listen, Father. The private investigation into the poor boy's murder is going well. Of course the welfare of the boy's family is at the forefront of everything; the parents have been informed, and reassured that justice will be served."

Father Mathers nodded sagely.

"I've just been rather concerned," Cardinal Moore went on. "About the poor nun who found the boy's body. What was her name?"

"Sister Veronica, Your Eminence. I was actually going to speak to -"

"Ah, yes, Sister Veronica." The Cardinal cut him off. "She was so distraught, was she not? So traumatised by her finding? And understandably so. She's a woman, a being with a sensitive soul."

Father Mathers nodded slowly. As well as a stab of irritation at not being able to fully explain and take credit for his idea, he was beginning to think the Cardinal may have already thought along the same lines.

"Her near hysteria led me to believe, upon reflection, that in due course she may benefit from a rest somewhere," the Cardinal went on, his brow creased with concern. "I believe it is very relaxing in the north of England?"

Father Mathers nodded seriously.

"I had already thought," he couldn't help saying, "that the poor woman could also do with, er, unwinding somewhere very far from London."

"Ah, you know what they say about great minds," Cardinal Moore allowed his eyes to widen a fraction with conspiratorial suggestion. "Father Mathers, I believe you, with your understanding of the situation, are the perfect person to engage Mother Superior at the convent in a dialogue about Sister Veronica's health, forthwith. Of course, Sister Julia does not know about the boy, only about your carbon monoxide story, and that's all she needs to know. Please let her know that I've spoken to a convent in Cumbria, and that they will have room for Sister Veronica to join them in a week. Of course, this is in the poor woman's interests; she's suffered a terrible shock and needs to recuperate." He allowed himself a concerned frown. "Do pass on how concerned I was about the state of the poor nun's health when we visited the hostel to discuss a possible media engagement the other day. Positive promotion of the church is no longer a suitable possibility, of course, under present circumstances." The briefest glimmer of irritation flickered across his eyes. "Sister Veronica would clearly benefit from a permanent change of scene. Do you see?"

"Of course, Your Grace. It is my pleasure to serve you in any way I can. I have been very worried about Sister Veronica's health myself, and I am so pleased you are doing what is best for her."

"Excellent," Cardinal Moore stood up. "Your service has been noted and will be duly rewarded."

A thrill of delight ran down Father Mather's spine.

Chapter Twelve

That afternoon, at the same time as Father Mathers was hailing a taxi back to Soho – the Cardinal hadn't offered his private driver for the return journey - Sister Veronica rocked backwards and forwards as the underground train built up speed. Wedged into the narrow seat, unable to shift into a more comfortable position, she glared at the girl covered in tattoos opposite her. The girl shot her a kind smile before staring back at her phone. So she glowered instead at the adverts above the girls head. From the corner of her eye she detected a couple in a passionate embrace, swaying to and fro with the motion of the train. She hadn't been in a tube for a while, she'd forgotten about their all-pervading stink of grime.

On her way into the tube station she'd passed a rack of daily newspapers, and caught a small headline on the front of The Telegraph: *"Cardinal Moore Promises Clerical Celibacy Will Never End"*. Why say such a thing? Why was the man so against change? She couldn't help feeling it was a message to Jamie's father and people like him. Or maybe to those in the Church who wanted the archaic rules relaxed.

Finding Melissa's address had been easy. As afternoon prayers began, she'd been in the convent office, snooping through the drawers, finding the book containing visitors contact details. Sister Irene's inevitable wrath at her lack of appearance in prayers, and Mother Superior's inevitable despondent disappointment in her when Sister Irene complained, were no longer future events she cared about.

She was used to travelling on the underground of course, in fact she considered herself a dab hand at it and purposefully never looked at the tube maps as she passed them, choosing to turn her head nonchalantly the other way. Only Sister Irene, and until she was taken ill, Sister Anastasia, were virtual prisoners inside the convent. Sister Irene out of choice, she devoted her free time to prayer – apparently – and Sister Anastasia because she was wheelchair bound.

Patience and Saints preserve her, the rattling in this tube was enough to give anyone an aneurism. Why hadn't she had the intelligence to ask Melissa what she knew about Jamie's father when she'd had the chance?

"Excuse me," a wrinkled hand was laid on her arm. Sister Veronica snapped round to stare at its owner, who turned out to be a very old man. "I hope you don't mind me asking this," he went on, "but are you a nun?"

"Yes I am, as a matter of fact."

"I knew it! It was your cross and your sandals that gave you away. I'm a Catholic too, Sister."

Sister Veronica stared down at her plain brown sandals. She'd never considered them to be particularly "nunnish".

"I saw His Holy Father in Rome last year," the old man said with a nostalgic smile. "Best moment of my life."

Sister Veronica stared at him.

"The Pope truly is a gift from our heavenly father, isn't he?" The man went on. "All priests are really. I go and confess my sins every week, and I love absolution, when Father speaks for God, and tells me that God has forgiven me."

Is that really all it takes? Sister Veronica wondered, as the train wobbled round a sharp bend. Can someone just confess murder to God, and God forgives him? I fear we've stopped using our brains in this world.

Twenty minutes later she stood, wheezing heavily, outside a baby blue front door – 2B, Briar Mews - in Putney. Would the girl even open the door to her? There was only one way to find out. She rapped loudly, trying to shake off the unsettling feeling that she'd been followed since leaving the underground station. She'd looked around herself several times, and seen nothing suspicious. But still the feeling was there, an uneasy intuition. Hurry up and open the door, Sister Veronica muttered to herself. She knocked again.

Dash it all, what if the girl wasn't at home? Golly, where was that dreadful music coming from?

Chapter Thirteen

Melissa stretched a long, soapy, leg upwards. Although she'd been kicking herself for flouncing out of the convent, soaking in this hot bath covered in Laura Mercier honeyed bath foam felt bloody good. Some of the traumatic burden she'd carried since this morning was easing; not leaving at all, just settling into something more manageable.

Well, she thought, your resolve didn't last long, did it Melissa? One minute you were in it for the long haul, the next you storm out as soon as a nun says something you don't like. Grow up girl, it's about time. Knee-jerk reactions had always been one of her weaknesses.

After a few more minutes, she rinsed her hair, then stepped out of the bath, wrapping herself up in a freshly washed deep-pile towel. The smaller towel was wound round her head, turban-style.

She stared at herself in the mirror. Her spray tan was fading, and a new wrinkle had appeared. Other than that, things could be worse. She put her nose and eyebrow studs back in; banished during her time in the convent. Weird how it felt like a part of her was missing without them these days.

Going in to her bedroom, she grabbed her phone and thumbed through her playlist. What she needed was some loud Indie Funk. My Baby's In the Club soon swung through the room. As she pulled on her skinny jeans and thrust her feet into her pale blue sliders, she tilted her head. Was that someone knocking at her door? Bloody hell, whoever it was was giving her door knocker a run for its money.

She took a quick peek through the eye hole, then opened the door.

"Sister Veronica!"

"I was beginning to worry you weren't in," the old nun puffed, looking over her shoulder quickly.

"I'm so sorry -" Melissa started at the same time as Sister Veronica said,

"About this morning, I need to apologise."

They stared at each other and grinned, the air between them now peaceful. It felt good to be smile about something for a moment.

"Come in, Sister, come and have a cup of tea," Melissa held the door wide open. "I can't believe you travelled all the way out here to find me."

"Well," Sister Veronica tried to drag her gaze away from the newly arrived metalwork on Melissa's face. "There are lots of questions I need to ask you, my dear. I would love a cup of tea – three sugars – if you don't mind."

Melissa's ground floor apartment was small but stylish, Sister Veronica thought as she heard the girl flip the kettle on in the kitchen. She had a good look round at the pots of ferns, the large Liechtenstein pop art print on the wall, the two laptops – why did the girl need two? – both in baby pink, and the smart corner sofa suite. The walls, painted a pale teal colour, made the room soothing to be in. She was glad to see a well-stocked book shelf. Excellent. The girl was a reader. She'd been right to trust her.

Melissa smiled as she came back carrying two steaming mugs.

"Here you go," she placed one on the rosewood coffee table in front of the nun, before settling back into the armchair.

"Marvellous, thank you," Sister Veronica took a noisy sip. "Now, what I should have asked you earlier, but didn't, was what you know about the identity of Jamie's father?"

"Nothing, I'm afraid," Melissa's face creased with the effort of trying to recall any helpful information. "I literally just got a message from Children of the Ordained, that's the French support group, saying that Jamie Markham was the child of a priest and was in Westminster. The group might know more, though. Look, I'll show you their internet site."

She grabbed one of the pink laptops and pulled up a webpage.

"Look, Sister."

The old nun leaned forward and took the laptop.

"And you're in touch with this group?"

"Yes, I speak to the founder a few times a week. He's been great actually."

"Do you think you could introduce me to them? We need to find out as much as we can about Jamie, and the most key information is about his father. I can go and talk to his mother, of course, but I have a feeling the Cardinal will have silenced the woman somehow."

"Sister," Melissa said. "Have you considered that maybe Jamie was killed by someone unconnected to the church?"

"Yes, yes I have, that is a real possibility," Sister Veronica shook her head. "But I just can't fully accept it as a probability. It seems too much of a coincidence that he'd come to find his father here, that it was a secret he was planning to share."

A thought occurred to Melissa, and she mulled it over for a second or two.

"Er, Sister Veronica," she said. "This might sound a bit much, but my brother – also adopted - lives in Paris. He's an artist in residence at a gallery there."

"The Louvre?" Sister Veronica's eyes widened.

"No, he's good but he's not that good," Melissa smiled. "He works in a smaller gallery in Montmatre. Now, I haven't told my editor that I've left the convent yet, so I'm basically a free woman for the next four days, until Monday. I know it's probably a crazy idea, but we could get a Eurostar over to

Paris and I could introduce you to the group. I've always wanted to meet them in person." And I could do with getting away for a day or two, she added privately. I need to get some perspective on all this craziness. "If they have any documents about him, like copies of birth certificates, photos, or anything, then they will be able to show you in person. They always ask each priest or nun's child for as much information as possible."

Sister Veronica frowned.

"Just go to Paris?" She was trying to work out the logistics. Easter week was out of the way – it had come early this year - so she had no pressing responsibilities other than her normal chores. And now that the students in the Catholic hostel had been rehoused...

"It would be helpful, vital in fact, to see any documents that connect Jamie with his father," she said. "But I don't know if Mother Superior would grant me permission, after all she doesn't know that Jamie is dead and on no accounts can I tell her. And I'm not exactly her favourite person, Sister Irene makes sure of that."

"Oh, Sister Irene, she's hard work isn't she?" Melissa rolled her eyes. "She kept telling me that a woman's place is in the home, not out at work."

Sister Veronica grimaced.

"I tell you what," she said. "Can you let me mull the Paris idea over for a day or two? Are you sure your brother won't mind? If you give me your number I'll see what I can do about getting permission to leave for a couple of days, but I have a feeling it won't come to pass."

Melissa took her notebook out of her handbag, wrote her number down, trying to ignore the slight pang of disappointment she felt. For a moment, she'd been visualising herself and Sister Veronica zooming over to Paris - travelling first class of course. But of course in reality Sister Veronica couldn't just up and leave on a whim. After all, she – Melissa – might be able to extract any information that they needed from the support group's founder over the phone. Perhaps that's what her new friend was hoping for but was too polite to ask. She ripped out the page from her notebook, and Sister Veronica folded it and put it in the depths of her carrier bag.

"No, Sean won't mind, he's always trying to get me to go and visit, but I keep saying I'm too busy," she smiled.

She watched Sister Veronica thumb through the pages of the black diary she'd retrieved from her bag.

"Melissa, this is Jamie's diary," Sister Veronica said. "I took it out of his room after I knew the Cardinal was going to try and cover up his murder. On the day he was killed, Jamie was expecting me to come over and bake my usual cake. All it says on that day, is "Today's the day: Tell Sister Veronica." What do you think he meant by that?"

"I reckon he was planning to tell you about his father," Melissa said. "It's a big deal being the child of a priest or a nun, it's like you have to come out about it to your friends and family who don't know. My friend Andre, from the group, is also the child of a priest, and he said it was easier to come out as gay to his friends than it was to tell them about his dad."

Sister Veronica nodded, her jowly cheeks wobbling.

"Yes, I felt he was going to disclose information about his father to me too," she said. "In his room, he had so many packets of pills. Do you know what Sertraline is? Or what Lithium is used for?"

"Sertraline is an antidepressant," Melissa said. "The doctor put me on it once a few years ago when the relationship with my adoptive mum started going bad. I just felt so low at the time."

"Oh dear that sounds most wearisome," Sister Veronica took a swig of her tea. "Are things better now?"

"I'm not depressed anymore, Sister, if that's what you mean. But no, my mother and I don't talk. She knows who my birth mother is, but she's refusing to tell me because she doesn't want me to make trouble for the church. She'll protect them at all costs," Melissa looked down. "That's one of the reasons Sean went to France, he can't handle her either. She's so miserable about everything all the time."

"Well she's lucky to have a daughter like you," Sister Veronica said stoutly.

Melissa smiled.

"I've never taken Lithium, but I think it's used to help people with bi-polar disorder," she said. The nun looked blank. "Manic depression," Melissa added. There was no way she was going to tell the old girl about all the less legal chemicals she'd experimented with at uni.

"Oh poor boy, he was in a bad way," Sister Veronica shook her head sorrowfully. "Is there anything else, anything at all that you can think of that might help Jamie?"

"Only putting you in touch with the support group," Melissa said. "Sorry Sister, I keep kicking myself for not going to see him earlier. But if anyone knows anything about him, it will be Children of the Ordained. I'll phone them and see if they'll talk to you."

She reached for her mobile and found the number. It rang and rang.

"There's often no answer during the day," she said. "All the people who work at the group hold down jobs and run the group in the evenings. I'll keep trying."

She saw the old nun glance at her digital wall clock.

"I must be going," Sister Veronica said. "I want to pop in at the hospital on the way back and see Sister Anastasia. The poor thing collapsed the other day, it must be the heat. And I need to get back before dinner, Sister Irene is going to make such a fuss as it is." She heaved herself up.

"You've got my number," Melissa didn't want the nun to go, she realised. It felt safer with her there. "Call me if I can help at all, OK?"

"Thank you, you've been so helpful already my dear. If your support group will talk to me, please call the convent office and leave a message for me to phone you back. Walls have ears in that place, one can never be too careful. If the group have any information about Jamie at all, it would be marvellous." Sister Veronica turned and waved a hand the size of a slab of meat. "Look after yourself, and put that chain on your door at night."

Chapter Fourteen

The interior of Westminster's Holy Cross Chapel was cool and dark. Bishop Hammett walked down the aisle and round the apse, not giving one glance to the glazed depictions of saints in the stained glass windows. He'd studied hundreds of times before. Today, his destination was the intricately carved confessional near the crypt.

He entered the small, dark space, knelt, and made the sign of the cross, feeling tears already wetting his eyes.

"Bless me, Father, for I have sinned," he said to the obscured latticed window. Only a silhouette and a grunt confirmed the presence of the other. "It has been three days since my last confession, and again, I want to declare my weakness, for it is a weakness, for the flesh of another."

Another grunt.

"I confess that I have had impure thoughts about this person, and some acts of togetherness with them."

A moment of silence from the other side. Then a man's voice spoke;

"The flesh is weak, Father. You must pray to the God almighty for guidance and strength, it is the devil throwing temptation in your path."

"I will," Father Hammett was sobbing now. "I will continue to pray. But Father, I don't have the strength to resist. My God, I am sorry for my sins with all my heart. In choosing to do   wrong and failing to do good, I have sinned against you who I should love above all things. I firmly intend, with your help of course, to do penance, to not sin anymore, and to avoid whatever leads me to sin. Our Saviour Jesus Christ suffered and died for us. In his name, my God, have mercy."

He heard a sigh. Then the unseen man spoke again;

"I see. God, the Father of mercies, through the death and resurrection of his Son has reconciled the world to himself and sent the Holy Spirit among us for the forgiveness of sins, through the ministry of the Church may God give you pardon and peace, and I absolve you from your sins in the name of the Father, and of the Son, and of the Holy Spirit. Go in peace."

"Thank you, Father. Thanks be to God," Bishop Hammett crossed himself and stood up.

Calmer now, forgiven, he walked back up the same aisle, his head bowed. He crossed himself again before leaving the chapel.

Blinking, as the bright sun hit him, his thoughts turned to Father Mathers. He'd been concealed in a side room when the man had arrived at the Archbishop's House yesterday. He'd seen him of course, through the crack in the door. He'd almost been able to smell the odour of pompousness that the man carried around with him like a bad aftershave. Although he didn't like the ferrety faced priest, he felt he should be almost grateful to him. After all, he'd been an unexpected decoy, allowing Father Hammett to gain access to strictly confidential information.

It had been unusual for His Eminence to leave such a private folder on his desk, usually everything of significance was locked in his impenetrable filing cabinet. Bishop Hammett supposed it was the early arrival of Father Mathers that had thrown His Grace somewhat, making him exit his office with haste. Of course he – Bishop Hammett – had looked through the file, making sure the door was firmly shut first. Sister Bernadette was the Cardinal's personal sniffer dog. The contents had not surprised him; after all he was a priest with as much complex knowledge of the secret Catholic underworld as most who'd risen to his station. The information had been helpful though. He now knew what he needed to do next.

Chapter Fourteen

Shifting her carrier bag to the other hand, Sister Veronica entered South Kensington's hospital, St Georges, the smooth sliding doors closing neatly behind her. Sweating profusely, she thanked God for the chilled air that immediately surrounded and cooled her. She looked up as thunder cracked overhead; she'd made it just in time to miss the rain.

The astonishingly young receptionist – she didn't look a day over sixteen - sent her off towards Sister Anastasia's ward with a thin-lipped smile. Approaching the old nun's bed, she saw a most welcome figure already there, head bowed in prayer.

"Father John!"

"Sister, at last! I was hoping to see you," his kind eyes wrinkled as he looked up. "How on earth are you after the whole carbon monoxide affair? Please, have this seat."

After they'd exchanged pleasantries, and Father John had gone off in search of a second uncomfortable chair, Sister Veronica bent over Sister Anastasia. She was shocked at what she saw. The old nun was asleep, God bless her, her pallid face sunken unusually at one side. Someone had taken her habit off, and her sparse white hair stuck up in tufts all over her head.

"The doctor said she's suffered a stroke," Father John said as he returned, placing a chair down. "He said this often happens to very old people in strong heat. She's been asleep for most of the time I've been here, poor old Anastasia."

They bowed their heads, Sister Veronica praying fervently that her Sister felt no pain.

"Father Mathers was in full micro-managing mode the other day," Father John smiled after a few moments. "He sent me away like a naughty school boy, told me not to ask any questions."

Sister Veronica couldn't help smiling.

"I can quite imagine him doing that. That man's a menace." Then she looked away, wishing she could tell her friend more. She was glad to see him, but at the same time it made her feel lonely, reinforcing the fact that she had to carry the burden of Jamie's murder silently.

"Are you alright, Veronica? You look sad," Father John leaned forward, concerned. "I know you well enough to know when something's up. Sister Irene's not being difficult again is she?"

"Oh it's just -" Sister Veronica began, then stopped. "I just feel let down by something, John. And I've had a busy day in this sweltering heat. It all gets a bit much for an old goose like me."

"Let me find you some water." Father John stood up and went off on his mission, she heard him asking one of the nurses if there was a water cooler about.

Sister Anastasia made a gurgling noise, bringing Sister Veronica to her feet at once.

"Hello, my dear. It's me, Veronica. How are you today?" She stroked a tuft of the old nun's hair. Sister Anastasia's blind eyes opened.

"I know," the nun whispered. At least that's what it sounded like, her speech was so slurred.

"What do you know?" Sister Veronica asked, bending down.

The old nun's mouth moved in a variety of directions as she tried to form words.

"I know," she repeated at last. "Wha happened tha day."

Sister Veronica's heart lurched. She immediately thought of Jamie, then berated herself for linking everything with him. The old nun was probably just confused. But what if she was trying to tell her something significant? This would be her only chance to find out. Her brain raced; where had Sister Anastasia been at the time of his murder? She didn't know the precise time the boy had been killed, but he'd been alive that morning – the other hostel students had told Melissa they remembered seeing him. And she'd found him dead at half past three. She remembered hearing voices in the convent garden as she got the cake ingredients together in the kitchen, and she recalled thinking that one or other of the Sisters usually wheeled Anastasia into the garden to sleep in the sun.

"What happened with what?" Sister Veronica asked, looking around, hoping the old nun would speak again before Father John got back.

Again, her mouth made shapes, her lips pressed together. She was desperately trying to say something. Sister Veronica leaned forward even further.

"M-m-m-m-murder," Sister Anastasia said slowly. Then her eyes closed.

"Here we are," Father John said cheerfully, as he victoriously carried in two plastic cups of water.

"Thank you, John," Sister Veronica said distractedly, her mind working overtime.

"Did she say anything while I was gone?"

"What? Oh, no, no, just some gurgling noises," Sister Veronica said, taking a quick sip of water. "I think she's gone back to sleep. I must go now, John, or Sister Irene will have me hauled up in front of the Cardinal for negligence of my vows."

Father John smiled.

"It's been good to see you, Veronica," he said. "Take care of yourself, you look tired."

Fifty minutes later, Sister Veronica trudged heavily down Soho Street towards Soho Square Gardens. The storm had passed, leaving a pale dusky sky in its wake. All she could do, she considered, glancing at a wispy white cloud, was to carry on, do her best for Jamie, and hope and pray that things got easier from here. It would be some consolation to help bring justice for Jamie, if indeed she could.

As she neared the intersection, a woman came towards her.

"Sister Cecelia?" Sister Veronica was surprised, but she was so tired she could hardly get the words out. "What are you doing here?" Sister Cecelia worked for the Cardinal in Archbishop's house. She'd always seemed like a downtrodden doormat, unlike that Sister Bernadette.

"I've been asked to deliver this to you," the nun thrust forward a white envelope. Sister Veronica looked at the writing on the front. It was written in capitals, but the handwriting still looked vaguely familiar. She ripped it open, pulled out the folded white sheet, and read; "SISTER VERONICA, I WRITE TO YOU AS A FRIEND. INFORMATION HAS COME TO ME THAT CARDINAL MOORE IS PLANNING TO HAVE YOU MOVED TO A CLOSED CONVENT IN THE NORTH. HE IS WORRIED YOU MIGHT TALK ABOUT THE AFFAIR WITH JAMIE MARKHAM. FATHER MATHERS HAS BEEN SPEAKING TO SISTER JULIA ABOUT IT, THIS AFTERNOON. I URGE YOU TO HASTILY REHOUSE YOURSELF BEFORE THIS HAPPENS, JUSTICE NEEDS TO BE SERVED. FROM, A CONCERNED SYMPATHISER".

"Who gave you this?" Sister Veronica demanded sharply. But Sister Cecelia shook her head as she scurried away. She stared back at the note. Dash it all, where did she recognise that writing from? Someone with inside knowledge wrote this, but it wasn't the Cardinal or Father Mathers, that was for sure, and apart from Melissa and herself she hadn't thought anyone else knew about Jamie. But the tangled secret web of the church's underbelly was obviously more complex than she knew. So many secrets and so many lies, it was disturbing. Whoever it was seemed to want to help her, and they had given her an idea.

As she entered the convent the first thing she saw was Sister Irene's intensely smug face. How long had the old goat been standing there?

"Mother Superior would like to see you in her office, Sister. Now."

Sister Veronica entered the office and sat down in the worn-looking swivel chair opposite Sister Julia.

"Sister Veronica," Sister Julia's serious face studied her own. "Today has been full of people giving me reports about you. First Father Mathers tells me that both himself and His Eminence are concerned that you are under undue mental stress, following your recent meeting with them. Apparently you exhibited near hysterical behaviour, although I find this hard to imagine. Then Sister Irene tells me that not only have you have missed yet another prayer meeting, but that you left the convent today without asking permission, and were gone for hours." She stopped, considering the hot-looking, dishevelled nun before her for a moment. "Well?" She said. "What have you got to say by way of explanation for all this?"

"I went to see Sister Anastasia in hospital this afternoon," Sister Veronica said, quite truthfully, trying not to focus on the severity behind the words the old nun had uttered to her until she'd left the meeting. "Father John was there. I'm sorry I didn't ask your permission, Sister, but the urge to visit Anastasia overtook me just as afternoon prayers were beginning, and I decided to follow my instincts and go. I was very anxious to see her soon, just in case her condition worsened and I didn't get another chance."

"I see," Sister Julia's shoulders stayed tense. "And this nonsense about you being hysterical?"

"I honestly don't know what they mean by that," Sister Veronica said. "All I did that day was help Father Mathers pack up the students' belongings, and I did that very calmly, in my opinion." She smiled.

Sister Julia sighed. Sister Veronica had never seen her look so concerned.

"Veronica, this isn't the first time we've had a chat like this, is it?"

"No, Sister."

"I don't know what you've done to get on His Grace's radar, but whatever it is, I would suggest you stop it at once. Father Mathers – quite enthusiastically in my opinion – said that His Grace thinks it would be better to move you out of London, perhaps to a calmer setting in the north of England. It would be better for your nerves, apparently. You need to understand that as His Grace has decided this, it's out of my hands completely. You have to go, do you understand? I'm sorry, Veronica. Please behave with obedience from now on."

"Yes, Mother Superior," Sister Veronica said, standing up. "Thank you, I understand."

Up in her room, Sister Veronica rooted through the mess at the bottom of her cupboard.

A week? The Cardinal was moving her to an obscure convent in a week? Oh no, absolutely not. He wasn't getting rid of her that easily, thank you very much. She finally located her old satchel under a pile of winter clothes. Into it, went clothes, Jamie's diary, the stash of money she'd secretly been hoarding to buy books with, her passport – applied for three years ago when she'd gone to spend six weeks in a convent in Nairobi - two full packets of Custard Creams, a pen, and the piece of paper with Melissa's number on it.

She made a great show of being at dinner that evening, chatting to Sister Mary about Nigeria, smiling at Agnes, ignoring Sister Irene, filling everyone in on the fact that poor Sister Anastasia had suffered a stroke and that when she'd left Father John had been there, watching over her and praying.

The nuns generally went to bed early; they were all required to rise at dawn for morning prayers. By half past nine, everything was quiet. If the nuns weren't asleep, they were resting in their rooms. Sister Veronica picked up her satchel and her coat, and descended the stairs with what she hoped was stealth. Most of the lights in the halls were out, just the stairwell strip lighting cast dim hospital-like illumination down the corridors. Gentle snoring came from one of the rooms.

Achieving the ground floor without hearing anyone stir, Sister Veronica tiptoed into the office and placed a note on Mother Superior's desk. Then she unbolted the front door as quietly as she could, knowing the Chubb lock would automatically click and keep the Sisters safe when she shut it again.

Setting off at an unusually smart pace, Sister Veronica headed up Soho Street towards London's busy Oxford Street. She veered off into a busy café, and swung her crucifix out of her shirt so it was noticeable.

"Excuse me," she shouted to the Polish waitress, desperate to be heard above the pounding music and rowdy customers. "I'm from the convent in Soho Square Gardens. Our phone is broken, and one of the Sisters has been taken ill. Could I possibly use your phone for a moment?" Honestly Veronica, she warned herself, as she watched the waitress grab a phone. You'll be as bad as Father Mathers if you become any more proficient at lying. She had Melissa's number ready in her hand. Taking the phone into a corner of the café, she tapped the numbers in.

"Hello, Melissa? It's Sister Veronica. Something's happened. Yes I'm fine. I can't explain at the moment but I would now most definitely like to take you up on your idea of going to Paris."

Chapter Fifteen

Father Mathers' fingers drummed out an agitated beat on the back of the chair. He watched a series of muscles twitch down both sides of the Cardinal's face.

"Missing?" Cardinal Moore hissed. "What do you mean, Sister Veronica is missing? How can a nun go missing?"

"I don't know, Your Grace. Like I said, Sister Julia telephoned me this morning in a panic. They've looked in Sister Veronica's room, and some of her belongings have gone too." He tried to slow his breaths.

"Well where is she?"

"I-I-I don't know, Your Eminence."

Father Mathers had to endure the sight of Cardinal Moore's lip curling contemptuously.

"This is your responsibility, Father," Cardinal Moore's dark eyes lazered into his. "All I asked you to do was to watch the nun and make sure she behaved. And now you tell me she's gone missing? This is not good enough. Find the woman. And bring her to me with the utmost urgency. Today. I have a pressing engagement in Rome that I cannot miss, and my flight leaves this evening. I want this disastrous matter cleared up well before that. Things will turn most unfortunate for you if you fall short this time. Do you understand?"

"Of course, Your Grace. I'm so sorry."

"Then why are you still standing here?" The Cardinal's face twisted and he banged his fist on the desk. The controlled, sophisticated man had morphed into a tower of aggression, spittle wet his lips and his eyes blazed with fury.

"GO!" Cardinal Moore snarled. "What the hell are you waiting for, man?"

Father Mathers ran his tongue round his dry mouth as he hurried out. It wasn't just Cardinal Moore that terrified him, it was also the much unwanted information Bishop Hammett had hissed into his ear on the way up. The

Bishop's instructions had been unthinkable, but what else was he supposed to do?

Chapter Sixteen

Melissa's feet tapped on the floor of the train, urging it to go faster. She stared through the window at the Paris suburbs, which were a more comforting sight than Sister Veronica's depressed face opposite her.

She couldn't deny that she'd felt a thrill of excitement when Sister had phoned last night, she'd felt like she was in an action-adventure film. Let's jump on a train to Paris? Sure, she could make that happen. She'd always been good at flying by the seat of her pants, that was one of the things that made her such an agile journalist; she'd throw herself into anything. A few phone calls later, she'd met Sister Veronica by the Clock Tower at Kings Cross, they'd spent the night in a twin room in the Travelodge, discussing Sister Anastasia's revelations into the early hours, then had made it on to the Eurostar from St Pancras by half past seven that morning.

She sighed, tucking some strands of hair behind her ears. This would almost be fun if the purpose of their mission wasn't so awful, and if Sister Veronica wasn't so moody.

"A week, Melissa." Sister Veronica said, yet again. Her eyebrows were so low they'd almost eclipsed her eyes. "The man was going to transfer me in a week. Without consulting me, taking me away from everything and everyone I know. And him, a man of God!"

"It's just not fair, Sister," Melissa soothed. "But he won't get the chance now, you're with me now, and we are doing this for Jamie, aren't we? My brother said he's looking forward to meeting you. Children of the Ordained are based fairly close to where he lives, just a couple of stops away on the Metro. They said they will be happy to talk to you, they were horrified to hear what's happened to Jamie."

Sister Veronica's eyes darted to and fro as the train zoomed on.

"This church has evil at its core, Melissa."

"Yep," Melissa agreed. "I think lots of people see that, Sister. The way it tried to cover up the clerical sexual abuse crisis was terrible, I wrote an article about it. Lots of bishops and cardinals knew these children were being hurt but they did nothing to help them."

"I thought the men who committed those crimes were bad apples," Sister Veronica said. "I knew there was corruption, but I thought it was contained, and getting better now that it was so public. But now I'm beginning to wonder whether that was just the tip of the iceberg. All these underhand dirty dealings, it's like the Mafia."

"Apparently the Vatican Bank does have links with the Mafia, I read that when I was writing the article," Melissa said. "But there are hundreds of good people like you in the Church too, Sister. Don't forget that."

"Yes, most of the people I know in the Church are good people," Sister Veronica said. "But they are not the ones who hold the power, they are just following their vocations, trying to do their best, believing the drivel that those in power put out – poor beggers - when in actual fact what seems to be happening is the cover ups of crimes. And they are crimes," she added vehemently. "I don't care what the Cardinal says about sin, abuse and murder are crimes and it's not right to keep them secret just to save the face of an institution that clearly has corruption at its core. I'm no longer working for the Catholic Church, I'm working for God. And they are two very different things."

Melissa nodded. She had grown very fond of this old lady over the last twenty four hours. There was something very refreshing about Sister Veronica's ability to stare a problem in the face and honestly address it even when her view contrasted with her institution's.

"No one's pulled the wool over your eyes yet though, have they Sister?" She glanced out of the window. "Ooh look, we're coming into Paris. Won't be long now."

Chapter Seventeen

The chairman of Soho's parish church council, Martin O'Hara, St Joseph's paced the room. Why the fuck wasn't that priest Mathers answering his phone? He was late to their meeting, again. Would he fail to turn up, like last time? Mathers' recent behaviour was of grave concern to Martin. They'd done a deal, all in good faith, a little transfer of funds that benefited both of them and hurt no one. Martin had come good on his half, and Mathers had reaped the rewards, lots of them. But why wasn't he fulfilling what he'd promised? He'd left Martin in the shit and now pressure was mounting, the bursar had mentioned that there was a problem with the books, that the funds no longer added up. If there was an investigation there was no way he was going to take the rap for the priest, no way.

It was only half past ten, but Martin took his flask out of his bag and took a deep draught of scotch. He badly needed something to take the edge off, to calm his nerves. If he went down, the priest was sure as hell coming with him.

He reached for his phone, Mathers number was at the top, of course. He tapped the button, listened, but the phone just rang and rang. He gulped more of his drink. He'd been waiting for Mathers for forty five minutes. The priest wasn't coming, he could feel it in his bones.

Right. He'd had enough of the lying bastard. Time to take matters into his own hands.

Chapter Eighteen

"Can we call in on Mark before we go to the offices?" Melissa asked, as they exited the Gard du Nord, breathing in the hustle and bustle of Paris life.

"Of course, let us go right away, is your brother expecting us?"

"I phoned and left a message," Melissa smiled.

The taxi bombed through the crowded streets and Sister Veronica's breathing slowed as the distraction of Paris temporarily overtook her frazzled mind. As they alighted onto a cobbled street, she looked up at the beautiful terraced houses towering over the boulevard. Lines of washing fluttered over their heads and music and raised voices floated above the beeps from the now gridlocked traffic around them.

"He is on the third floor of this one." Melissa pointed to an old wooden double door, with a line of bell pushes beside it.

She rang one and they heard a distant jangle.

"Oui?" a voice from above them called down.

"Mark, it's me!" Melissa stepped back into the street.

"Sis!" Come on up, the door is open."

The next half an hour became a blur of steep steps, joyful introductions, hastily assembled refreshments, admiration of abstract paint splattered depictions of the River Seine, and the alarming realisation that they were very soon due in nearby Notre Dame de Lorette. Ten minutes later, after a crowded Metro ride, Sister Veronica found herself seated in the shabby office rented by Children of the Ordained, quickly orientating herself.

She put down the fresh mug of coffee Melissa pushed into her hands and stared in to Dominique Caron's beautiful, serious face.

"Thousands of priests and nuns children?" She repeated. "All over the world? Are you sure?"

"Very sure, Sister," Dominique said in her lilting English accent. "We have been running this group for three years now, and we have evidence to show this. Thousands is a conservative estimate. In many countries like Nigeria and the Philippines, the priests have more than one child and live quite openly with them. The real number is probably nearer tens of thousands."

"But why doesn't the world know about this?" Sister Veronica's brow furrowed.

"Because the church and their mothers and fathers, and also communities, silence them. They usually believe they are doing the best for the child."

Sister Veronica nodded. She was thinking back to her own mother's words, "We must protect the church's good name, Veronica... Just forget you ever found out, put it out of your mind, do you hear? I never want to hear another word about this."

"Yes," she nodded slowly. "Yes, I see."

"Jamie's case was text book," Dominique shook her head. "He found out he'd been lied to all his life, that his real father was a priest, that he'd been fed made up stories about his heritage just so his father could continue to be seen to be celibate. Unfortunately his mental health was very fragile. It all got too much for him and he tried to commit suicide. Unfortunately this is normal for priests' children. The data we have, and the data we've been given from other countries, suggests that over fifty five percent of priests' and nuns children will attempt suicide during their lives."

Sister Veronica let the shock pass through her body.

"But why?" she asked. "That number is staggeringly high."

"Yes, it is," Dominique agreed. "There are a number of risk factors for priests and nuns' children that contribute towards this. If someone has too many of these factors they are statistically more likely to attempt suicide or have suicide ideation. Poor Jamie had lots of these. He was once very devoutly Catholic you know, so when he found out he felt the attached shame and stigma very strongly, he internalised it. He was lied to, his father rejected him. The church closed doors in his face when he went to them for help."

Sister Veronica shook her head.

"This is inexcusable," she said. "Children should not be born into this."

"I absolutely agree with you, Sister Veronica," Dominique said. "The church is known to have gone to extreme lengths to stop priests and nuns' children from finding out about their parentage. We've been shown evidence of court cases, confidentiality agreements, destroyed birth certificates, upon lie upon lie. All to make priests and nuns appear celibate when they are not, and this is all to protect the good name of the church. Celibacy is one of the tenets that the church rotates around. If they are seen to be failing at this, the whole structure of it falls down. They are prepared to keep the image of priests and nuns being collectively celibate at all costs."

Sister Veronica snorted.

"But murder?" She said. "Have you seen that before?"

"I've heard of cases," Dominique said darkly. "Have you seen the documentary series called The Keepers? It's on Netflix."

"What is Netflix?" Sister Veronica said.

"Ah, your mind is purer than mine, Sister," Dominique said. "Netflix is a streaming service for televisions and other digital devices like laptops. You can watch films and documentaries on it. I have to admit I watch it quite often in the evenings."

"Me too," Melissa said. "I'm addicted." Dominique smiled at her.

documentary series about the unsolved
Cathy Cesnik, who strongly believed a priest
taught in had committed awful sexual
abuse crimes. Many people believe that Sister Cathy was murdered to silence her, to stop her talking about what the priest had done, and that the church covered this up. So you see, there are people in the church who are prepared to go to extraordinary lengths to stop certain truths being said about them."

Sister Veronica could feel the blood draining from her head. A dizziness took over and she shut her eyes.

"Are you alright, Sister?" Dominique's voice was full of concern. "Have some of your coffee, the sugar in it will help you."

Sister Veronica picked up her mug and drank. The room swam back into focus. She patted her pocket, trying to locate her emergency bag of Custard Creams.

"I've told you everything I know about Jamie's murder," she said. "As you can see, we still don't know who did it, whether it was someone in the church or outside."

"True," Dominique nodded. "But what you do know the highest authorities are covering up his murder. I would they do that?"

They sat in silence for a minute.

"Who was really was Jamie, Dominique?" Melissa asked. "Do you have any more information about him that might help us?"

"I have his file here," Dominique opened the plain file in front of her. "We assign numbers to each priest or nuns' child's file, to help with confidentiality. Jamie was number 9453. The information we have about him is sparse, but I will tell you what we've got." She shuffled some papers. "It says here that he lived in Sidcup in Kent with his mother. He was attending Art College near there until his suicide attempt a year ago. He had found out about his real father by going through his mother's personal documents. She'd brought him up believing that his real father had died in a car crash before Jamie was born – maybe his mother wanted this to be true, it's much more straightforward. But he found her diary from the year before his birth and it details her relationship with a priest. No name, just the fact she was in a relationship with a priest when she was dying Theology at university. Jamie went to the church for help, he desperately needed to know who his father was. This is very common among priests and nuns' children, when they discover the lie they often develop an insatiable desire to know the truth of their parentage." Melissa nodded. "But the church didn't help him," Dominique went on. "He was at his wits end, when he received an anonymous letter a couple of months ago, from a "well-wisher", with the name of the person who had orchestrated the secrecy and silencing of Jamie and his mother."

"Who was it?" Sister Veronica asked sharply.

"I believe this man has been promoted since. But at the time of Jamie's birth, he was known as Father Henri Sabell."

"Bishop Sabell," Sister Veronica shook her head. "No wonder Cardinal Moore wants this covered up."

"Who's Bishop Sabell?" Melissa asked.

"Cardinal Moore's closest friend. They work together at The Archbishop's House," Sister Veronica frowned. "So let me check I've got the facts right," Sister Veronica said. "Bishop Sabell orchestrated the silencing of Jamie."

"Yes, he made Jamie's mother lie, he threatened her and said the bits of money she was being sent would stop if she ever spoke about the true identity of his father. She was scared of him," Dominique said.

"But he wasn't actually Jamie's father?"

Dominique shook her head.

"Then who was?"

Dominique spread her hands wide.

"Nobody knows," she said.

Chapter Nineteen

Cardinal Moore leaned back in his first class seat, considering his next move as the plane accelerated down the runway. The priest Mathers was a disastrous failure, there was no doubt about that. He hadn't even contacted the Cardinal to say he couldn't find the old goat Sister Veronica, sent no word, nothing. It was too bad. Unprofessional and unprincipled. Cardinal Moore ran a tight ship, and there was no room for this kind of inefficiency in it.

Of course he'd left Henri in charge of tracing the errant nun. Damn her. Things had been going so smoothly up till then. But she couldn't be far, and she wouldn't have much money with her. The senseless woman wouldn't be able to get up to much anyway, she didn't have the intelligence. He cast his mind back to how she'd snorted and cried at the sight of the boy's body. Typical female, driven by emotions not logic. She'd probably fled because she didn't want to be ensconced in the closed convent in Cumbria. When he found her, he'd make sure she never left the damn place. A life-long contemplation session should bring her to heel.

Sister Julia had phoned just as he was about to leave for the airport. Apparently the old nun Sister Anastasia had died in her sleep. Old age and a stroke. He'd given instructions for the funeral to be organised, and left them all to it. He had much greater things on his mind. He thought ahead to his meeting with Archbishop C, the... at the Vatican. There was some information he badly needed that would help with the investigation, bring it to a satisfactory close.

He shut his eyes; a caustic grimace remained etched on his face.

Chapter Twenty

It was the cleaner, Tina Naylor, who discovered Father Mathers' body, the little trickle of blood from his mouth dried almost black, his eyes wide and staring.

When the police got there she was white faced, dragging heavily on a cigarette, numbed with total shock.

"I aint touched nothing," she kept saying. "The room was messed up like this when I got here. And him such a tidy man. I just came in like usual and there he was on the floor. I mean, who would kill a priest?"

She had to stay there while the police took her witness statement, while the forensic team came in and combed through the room, scraping unseen things from the floor, putting clothes in bags, photographing Father Mathers' body from every angle.

"Burglary gone wrong?" She heard one of the officers ask the detective in charge.

"Mmm," was the dubious reply.

Chapter Twenty One

"What did you call this?" Sister Veronica gave a polite smile as she peered down her nose at the list in front of her. Dominique's colleague Victor Dubois had arrived with some information for her, She was touched by how they'd both taken time off work that day to talk to her. A young girl who'd been introduced to her as Simone, and who had extremely long legs that sported the shortest shorts Sister Veronica had ever seen, sat typing at a laptop laconically, chewing gum.

"It's a list of supporters," Victor said in broken English. "Simone just printed it out, she is the best assistant anyone could have." He smiled over at the girl and she winked back. "People all over the world who we have got to know, who help our mission."

"I see. And what exactly is your mission?" Sister Veronica asked.

Victor grinned. He had never met anyone quite like the old nun before.

"To help the children of priests' and nuns'. To support them, help them gain recognition from the Vatican, try and stop the shame, secrecy and stigma they are born in to. As I

believe Dominique has already told you, suicide a~
and mental illnesses are high among these peopl~
son of a nun myself, who understands exactly wh~~
like to be a living example of someone else's shame, it
makes me angry that so many people have to live with this.
It has to stop." Victor had stopped smiling. Passion now lit
his eyes. "Do you know what it is like to live with a secret
from the moment you're born, Sister? To have to lie, just so
someone else's lie can be upheld? To not know who you
really are, because your life has been twisted into a different
story by well-meaning people?"

Sister Veronica nodded slowly.

"Yes Victor," she said quietly. "Actually I do." A pain of
remembering how she'd been silenced and had to live a lie
ached through her, sharpening her devotion to finding out
what had happened to Jamie and if he'd been silenced to
help sustain a lie.

"Then you will understand why so many people feel so
strongly about this," he said. "I am a Catholic, Sister, and I
love my church. I would do anything for it. But these lies,
this mistreatment of children and adults in the name of God,
when God has nothing to do with this human-made mess,

to stop. Many priests and nuns, and members of the Roman Catholic Church feel the same. They want to help us too. They want their church to be a place of openness and peace, not one of dishonesty, fraud and vice. I mean, have you read the papers this morning?" Sister Veronica shook her head. "There was a front page piece about the head of a Catholic Church racketeering syndicate arrested in Chile. His name is Father Joaquin Vasquez. The article said they suspect this group is run within the Catholic Church remit all over the world, they just haven't been able to prove any other links. It's absurd, these crimes are always getting reported but it seems to make no dent on the Church, and it never cleans up its act at all. It's like it's invincible. You told us Cardinal Moore wants to have you moved to an obscure convent, Sister, to silence you. Does that not remind you of what happened to Sister Vincenza after she discovered the murdered body of Pope John Paul I in 1978? She was also silenced and moved far away. You see, there is a precedent here. They like to create a mafia-style omerta disguised as protocol."

Sister Veronica nodded sadly.

"Unlike the terrible crimes committed with clerical sexual abuse," Victor went on. "Where often it is just the priest and his victim who know the truth, with children of priests and nuns lots of people know the truth. You cannot easily hide a woman's pregnant belly. There are so many people complicit in this cover up it is unbelievable. But some of those people change their minds and come to us, saying they want to help. And that is what this list is, Sister. A register of all the names of people around the world who are helping us."

Sister Veronica nodded, acknowledging and feeling his desire to make the church a better place, his ache for positive change. Good. She was glad people like Victor and Dominique were there, helping and supporting these children, young and old. It was life-affirming to see positivity and compassion amid the dark chaos of murder and intrigue. Roman Catholic Church racketeering? Whatever next. She made a mental note to remember that for her next book, if she ever got a chance to write again, with all this bedlam.

Feeling rejuvenated by Victor's emotional speech, she scanned down the list of names. Each had a country attached to them; Sister Teresita – Philippines. Father Lopez – Mexico. Her keen eyes looked for British connections. She didn't recognise the first two, Father Barnes and Sister Ellen. But then a name caught her eye. She started in surprise.

"Bishop Christopher Hammett?" She said. "The same one who works in The Archbishop's House as the Cardinal's secretary?"

"The one and only," Dominique smiled, as Melissa came in carefully carrying a tray of freshly steaming mugs. "He has been part of our cause for two years now. And understandably so. He is a father himself, you know. Of a lovely girl who lives in England with his partner. He is torn up inside from trying to be a good priest, a good father and a good partner. I worry about him."

Sister Veronica's mouth was wide open.

"It's not often she's stuck for words," Melissa grinned, placing a mug of tea in front of the nun.

"Father Hammett wants to help you, Sister. He called me very early this morning. From what he said I understand he has some vital information that will help you. He's on his way to Paris now."

"Excellent," Melissa spoke for Sister Veronica, who was still digesting this latest revelation. Bishop Hammett? The father of a child? A supporter of Children of the Ordained? This whirlwind of discovery was taking some very unexpected turns indeed. "Will we have time for a late lunch before he gets here?"

Chapter Twenty Two

Before Cardinal Moore entered the restaurant, he made a phone call.

"Henri," he said, when a voice answered. "You know the man we spoke of before I left? No not Mathers, the other one. Yes, that's right. Have him watched, will you? Just a gut instinct. Oh, and tell the press to re-run the piece about clerical celibacy never ending. One more thing Henri, phone O'Hara. I had a jumbled voicemail from him, the man made no sense whatsoever." There was a short pause. "What do you mean something's happened?" There was a long pause. "Mathers? Thank you for this most interesting information. Oh and Henri, the Assessors will be back tomorrow, please make them feel welcome. God bless you too, Henri."

He smoothed down his shirt, and entered Le Felizianerie. Half empty, this middle of the road tourist destination was the perfect meeting place, he thought, satisfied. He saw his contact at once, and made his way towards him.

"How's the investigation going?" Archbishop Cancio, secretary of the Pontifical Council, asked as he sat down.

"Very well," Cardinal Moore answered, his eyes taking the contents of the menu in at one glance.

"I heard there might have been a little, how do you say, hiccup?" Archbishop Cancio smiled lazily, as if he'd just taken Cardinal Moore's queen in a chess game.

Cardinal Moore smiled back.

"Good news travels fast, I see, Matteo. Yes, we had a minor inconvenience but the team I have working on this now don't make mistakes. I made an error, which I am now fixing."

"Relax, Charles. I'm just teasing you, you should know me better by now," Archbishop Cancio poured another glass of wine and passed it to him. "I wanted to let you know that we've become aware of a little loose end of yours that floated over to the continent. Paris, to be precise. We are in the process of tidying it up for you."

Cardinal Moore stared at him, understanding.

"Thank you, Matteo. I will of course return the favour, should I ever need to."

"I know you will, I know you will," Archbishop Cancio sipped his wine. "Now, on to more important matters. As you know, the plan has unfolded in exactly the way we anticipated so far, and the next stage is starting soon. I've got some figures here for you." He took a folded piece of paper from his jacket pocket and handed it to Cardinal Moore. "Take a look."

The Cardinal unfolded the paper. He allowed his eyebrows to ascend a fraction of an inch. "This is impressive, Matteo. Over a billion. It's rising to levels even I hadn't predicted." He began shredding the paper into tiny bits.

"Yes, my friend, it is. And it will continue to grow, if we are wise and make the right decisions. Bishop Paulo Alfonsi from the Vatican Bank wants to talk to you and I this evening. A Sicilian by the name of Guglielmo Turatello will also attend. I said you would be there, si?"

"Of course." The men raised their glasses and toasted each other. Everything was about money and power, although neither would be so crass as to say such a thing. But these concepts, when made into realities, were the only things that ever ultimately mattered. That was the game.

"Actually, Matteo, there is something I need to ask you, to do with the other business. For the investigation to end in a satisfactorily final way, I need to see a copy of Nota relative alla prassi della Congregazione per il Clero a proposito dei chierici con prole. There's something I need to confirm regarding clerics with children, and possibly have – ah - amended. Could you do that for me?"

Archbishop Cancio regarded his compatriot as he took another sip of wine. He gave another lazy smile.

"For you, Charles, I can make that happen."

Chapter Twenty Three

"Sister, look!" Melissa was gesturing towards a newspaper stand. Sister Veronica was gazing longingly at a waiter deftly placing steaming plates before two hungry tourists. There was a relaxed feel in the Parisian streets, she'd noticed, despite the numerous people sitting at bistro tables or ambling about.

"What is it?" she called, edging closer to the nearest Brasserie's menu, posted neatly behind a glass screen near the café's door.

"Just come and look!" There was an edge to Melissa's voice. Sighing, and deeply inhaling the garlicky smell of moules et frites, Sister Veronica made her way to the newspaper stand.

"Oh my - " she stopped. Her body felt hot with rushing blood.

"*Breaking News: Money-Laundering Priest Found Dead At Home In London*" she read. "*Father Zachary St John Mathers, suspected of embezzling church-goers funds, has been found dead at his home in St Joseph's rectory in Soho. A post-mortem is being carried out to determine the cause of death. Police say their investigations are continuing. A spokesperson for the Roman Catholic Church, Bishop Sabell, has issued the following statement: 'We are greatly saddened to hear of the death of Father Mathers, and shocked by the allegations against him. We will continue to help the police in their investigations in any way we can.'"*

Sister Veronica felt sick. Another death, so soon after Jamie's. True, she hadn't liked the man at all, and she wasn't going to pretend she had now he was dead. But money-laundering priest? Embezzling church-goers funds? Like a whirring machine, information clicked into place in her head. The meeting she'd overheard in the convent, Father Mathers saying he needed more time. Had the foolish man really been trying to defraud honest church goers? But wait, the Cardinal had also asked him to keep an eye on her, she was sure of it. They way she'd heard them whispering that day at the hostel when she'd sneaked up to search Jamie's room. Was Father Mathers' death entirely unrelated to Jamie's murder? In these dark and twisted times it was hard to even guess.

"Are you OK, Sister?" Melissa put her hand on the Sister Veronica's shoulder. "You've gone very white."

"Yes, yes," she muttered. "Just a shock, that's all. Awful man, didn't like him a jot. But another death, what if it's somehow connected to Jamie?"

Melissa stared at the paper, reading through the article.

"Well," she considered. "The accusations of embezzlement against him point to his death possibly relating to that. Maybe he found out the papers had got hold of the story and took his own life? He came across as very arrogant sometimes, although I don't want to speak ill of the dead. He probably didn't want his reputation ruined. Or maybe someone he'd double crossed wanted revenge?"

Sister Veronica sighed.

"Yes, you're right, I shouldn't jump to conclusions." She shook her head, trying to clear it. "Right. Let's put that man out of our minds for now. Bishop Hammett will be meeting us soon and I don't know about you but I'm so hungry I could eat everything on that menu over there."

Chapter Twenty Four

Cardinal Moore's face had a hard edge as he pushed through the crowds in front of the Vatican's Sistine Chapel. Why weren't these people moving out of the way for him? Surely it was obvious who he was; the red and white robes more than gave it away. That was the problem with today's Catholics, they had no respect.

Several tourists milled around in front of its façade, hardly bothering to admire the fifteenth century restorations of Pope Sixtus IV.

"Philistines," the Cardinal muttered as he pressed past them and in to the interior of the chapel. He savoured the majestic artistic assault on his senses, letting the Renaissance masterpieces consume his attention for a minute or two. Then he walked to the back, tapping a code into a pad attached to an unassuming door. His destination was the usual private office he met his associates and business partners in, located two floors below the Papal Apartments.

As Cardinal Moore entered the meeting room, he saw three men sitting round the table. Matteo was already there.

"Ah, Your Eminence, welcome," Bishop Paulo Alfonsi was already on his feet, ushering the Cardinal towards an ornate chair. "Please, sit, sit. Here's some water, and some wine. You know His Grace already of course. Let me introduce our great friend Guglielmo Turatello, who travelled from Sicily to be with us today."

Turatello's moustache moved as his jowly face smiled, his chubby cheeks giving him a cherub-like look.

The men conversed in low voices for a while, catching up on news and sharing information.

"Gentlemen," Bishop Alfonsi's voice called the meeting to order. "Our scheme has gone well, as you all know. The new bonds from America are being trialled at the moment, if successful – and they will be – they will bring us a net profit of €900000 each. Your Eminence," he turned to the Cardinal. "A sample of the bonds will arrive in the UK tomorrow, going straight into The Wessex Building Society into the account you provided for us under the name Damien Hepworth. Please alert your contact to this, and ask him to observe and relay information after the bonds arrive and are processed. This will be the fourth and final trial before the main body of the bonds are invested through our partners in banks around the world."

Cardinal Moore inclined his head in acknowledgement.

"Guglielmo here has had the highest of, how shall we say, new bonds created for us," Bishop Alfonsi looked indulgently at the Sicilian. "We've been working together for many years. Never before did such a trusting partnership exist."

Achbishop Cancio chuckled.

"Of course in Chile, our partner – Father Joaquin Vasquez - was not so lucky. The story quite tickled me as I read the papers today," he said. "Racketeering, I believe, is the charge."

Bishop Alfonsi glared at the Archbishop.

"With respect, I arranged for that to happen, Your Grace," he said. "I had some documents about Vasquez leaked to the Chilean police, after I gained information that he was ciphering far more than his share off. Let it be a warning to our other partners around the world."

Archbishop Cancio clapped his hands.

"Oh, very good, very good," he laughed. "You're a smart man. I knew there was a reason I put you in charge of this."

As Bishop Alfonsi and Turatello fell into conversation about the bonds, Cardinal Moore leaned towards Archbishop Cancio.

"Have you managed to change what I asked on the document for clergy with children my friend?" He murmured.

"Of course, Charles. I added the information you gave me this very afternoon." Archbishop Cancio smiled languidly.

It was only because Cardinal Moore looked down at his watch at that moment, that he missed the look Bishop Alfonsi gave Archbishop Cancio, the nod he received in reply, and the small, knowing smile that then passed between them.

Chapter Twenty Five

Back out on the street again and blinking in the sun, their stomachs comfortably full, Sister Veronica and Melissa made their way to the front of the church of Notre Dame de Lorette. Standing in the shade in front of the huge stone pillars, Sister Veronica surveyed the busy urban landscape in front of her. Before Dominique and Victor had returned to their day jobs, the French woman had told them where to meet Bishop Hammett. He'd phoned just as they were leaving the office to say he was nearly there, and Simone had passed his message straight on.

Sister Veronica couldn't put her finger on exactly why she felt this, but she had an unshakeable conviction that they were being watched. It was the same feeling she'd had that day in Putney, when she was on her way to Melissa's apartment. Well nothing had come of that, so she was sure she shouldn't worry too much about this. Yet...

"Urgh," Melissa said, looking at her phone.

"Is there something wrong?" Sister Veronica asked.

"Oh, it's just my dick – my idiot ex-boyfriend," Melissa grimaced. "I've just got a text from him. He says he's sorry for the way he spoke to me the other day. He wants us to try again."

"And what do you want, Dear?"

"God knows," Melissa sighed. "I think I want to be with someone who really loves me, and doesn't want to change me."

"Well hold out for that then, Melissa. Don't compromise, you're a wonderful person. Wait for someone who can truly see that."

"Thank you Sister," Melissa shot her a grin, turning back to the crowds.

"Sister Veronica! And this must be Melissa?" Bishop Hammett strode towards them, his cleanly shaven face breaking into a smile. "How lovely to see you both."

"Bishop Hammett," Sister Veronica nodded, then introduced Melissa, who gazed at the man very coolly. She wondered whether the girl was having the same thoughts as her: how much could they trust this man? She gave an internal chuckle. From what Melissa had just said, it sounded like neither of them were very impressed with the men in their lives at the moment. Then she remembered Father Mathers, and the sick feeling returned.

"Shall we go somewhere more private to talk?" Bishop Hammett said, when the introductions and polite enquiries about travel had been made. "There's so much we need to discuss."

By the time they'd located a quiet space of grass down Rue de Chateaudun – Sister Veronica periodically checking over her shoulder - and settled down to talk, Bishop Hammett's smile had long since left, with well creased worry lines dominating his face instead.

"Yes, it's true I have a daughter," Bishop Hammett bowed his head. "God forgive me, I am weak when it comes to the flesh. But I love the Catholic Church and want to continue in my ministry. I know I can help people, but I love my daughter and my partner Anna, too. This conflict tortures me every day."

Sister Veronica's stiff posture relaxed as tears oozed out of the Bishop's eyes.

"Love, as St Paul said, is indeed the most important thing, Your Grace. It is very heart-warming to hear how much you love your child and partner and also the church," she smiled at him. "I am beginning to think that clerical celibacy is a myth, and that I am the only member of the cloth who is not a parent." Sister Veronica allowed herself a small chuckle. "The problem driving the whole terrible business of Jamie's life and murder, is the *absence* of love. When Jamie and other children of the ordained attempt suicide, I believe this is caused by their internalisation of shame. This is a lack of love not only from their fathers, and sometimes their mothers, but from the church – who often don't help them from what I've been told – from society, who read about scandalous naughty priest fathers being disgraced in newspapers, from friends and families who have helped silence the child by perpetrating the lie about their parentage. And this is all done to protect the *good* -" she spat the word, "name of the church. Do you see? These children, young and old, not only have to deal with all these lies and rejection, but come to terms that this is done in the name of God. It's alright if their fathers and mothers reject them, because it's what God wants. Well I'll tell you something, my God does NOT want children to be treated like this." Sister Veronica had fire in her eyes.

Bishop Hammett was nodding slowly, his tears drying on his cheeks. Melissa wrote feverishly in her notepad.

"And I'll tell you something else," Sister Veronica went on. "The ultimate antithesis of love was shown to Jamie; someone had the audacity to take away his most precious thing – his life. So you see, Your Grace," Sister Veronica leant her reddening face towards his. "I'm glad to hear of your love for your child and for the church. If more people were like you, we wouldn't be in this bloody mess."

She sat back, breathing deeply.

"Thank you, Sister," Bishop Hammett took her hands in his trembling ones. "Thank you. It has done me the world of good to hear your words. And I agree with every single one of them."

"But what I don't understand," Melissa looked up, laying down her pen. "Is why Cardinal Moore wanted to keep Jamie's death so secret. Why the big fuss? Why is he trying to send Sister Veronica away? Why not just let the police deal with it, it would be much easier for him."

"Ah, now that I may be able to help answer," Bishop Hammett's face was regaining colour, his voice now more self-assured. He reached into the inside pocket of his jacket and retrieved a folded piece of paper. "Before I show you this, let me explain something. As you will no doubt have heard from the hard-working Dominique and Victor, who have done so much for children of the ordained and their parents, there is a growing band of supporters of their work around the world."

170

Sister Veronica and Melissa nodded.

"Many are like me, they love their ministry but they see the mandatory clerical celibacy discipline as outdated and irrelevant in our modern times."

Sister Veronica snorted at the word "modern".

"These supporters come in all shapes and forms, some are lay people, some priests and nuns, some bishops like me, and some belong to the higher ranks in the church such as archbishops. We even have one or two Cardinals. And," he paused. "We have contacts in the Vatican itself. I spoke to one on the way here, and he is keen to help you. His contact details are on this paper."

He passed it to Sister Veronica. She opened it and read.

"But," Bishop Hammett went on. "The problem is that there is much evil in the church, as well as goodness. And unfortunately the epicentre of this is in the Vatican. There are several key players there who appear on the outside to be the most traditional members of the clergy, the best rule keepers, the dogma enthusiasts. But underneath, they are the biggest crooks and liars. I'm reliably informed that they have their fingers in an unbelievable amount of unsavoury pies. And many of them count Cardinal Moore as a very close friend. The way they have information at their fingertips is unbelievable. I have to warn you, Sister, that someone at the Vatican had already heard you were in France. The Catholic Church's upper echelons around the world are like a series of nosy villages. News gets passed from one to the other before the subject of the news has even got out of bed in the morning."

"What?" Melissa said. "Are you serious?"

"Deadly serious," Bishop Hammett said. "Sister Veronica, I cannot emphasise enough how fragile your safety is now. I'm sorry to say this, but you must be so careful. Trust lightly, and keep looking over your shoulder, as I saw you doing earlier. By finding Jamie's body, witnessing the Cardinal's response to it, being daring enough not to submit to His Eminence's instructions of being silenced far away in a closed order, and finally jumping ship to mount your own investigation – which, by the way, those at The Archbishop's House are convinced you're doing – you have come up as a glaring hazard light on the Vatican's radar, that some more corrupt inhabitants there believe must be eliminated. But there are very good people in power too, and the contact I've given you is one of them."

Sister Veronica stared at him.

"Have you heard about Father Mathers?" She asked.

Bishop Hammett shook his head.

"It's a terrible affair, the whole thing. I never took to the man myself, he was so full of himself. But to die before one's time is always a tragedy. We must commend his soul to the Lord. And also poor Sister Anastasia's soul, of course."

"Sister Anastasia?" Melissa asked, as Sister Veronica raised her eyebrows. "Has she passed away too?"

"Oh, haven't you heard? No, of course, you've been busy travelling. Yes, the poor thing passed away in her sleep yesterday evening."

Sister Veronica gazed into space.

"In my opinion," she said. "Either there is an unusual spate of unrelated deaths going on within the Diocese of Westminster, or there may be a serial killer on the loose. And that frightens me to the core of my being."

"But," Melissa said. "Sister Anastasia was very old, wasn't she? You said she'd had a stroke, it sounds like she died from natural causes."

"What caused the stroke?" Sister Veronica retorted bluntly. "When I went to visit her, she whispered in my ear that she knew what happened. She said the word murder. I am fully convinced that Sister Anastasia was in the convent garden at the time of Jamie's murder, and heard more than she could say. Don't forget, since going blind her hearing has sharpened. If only she could have told me more when I saw her that day. If only I'd known the right questions to ask her."

"I have to agree with you Sister, there are sinister goings on in Westminster at the moment," Bishop Hammett's face was grave. "I'm glad to be away from it. But like I said, be careful wherever you are these days."

Sister Veronica frowned at him.

"So what on earth are we going to do?" She asked.

"Dominique told me that the lovely Simone at their office has arranged for us to stay in a safe house near Paris tonight. It is at a convent full of sympathisers for the cause.

Tomorrow we travel to Rome, and meet the contact. He will know what to do, he will help you."

Melissa caught Sister Veronica's eye.

"Looks like we better get back to Sean's and pack our stuff up then?"

Chapter Twenty Six

"Melissa, write something down for me, please, would you?" Sister Veronica stared straight ahead, thinking hard. They were cruising along in the back seat of a cab, Bishop Hammett sitting next to the driver in the front. Unlike most of the taxi drivers Sister Veronica had spotted out of her window, their driver did not seem to have a death wish, and drove calmly and staidly, which pleased her immensely. Wiping crumbs from her shirt, the last remnants from the delicious baguette Simone had provided for the journey, she turned to look at her friend.

"Yup," Melissa fumbled for her pad and pen. "What do you want me to write?"

"I just want you to write down everything we know about Jamie and his death," Sister Veronica's eyes winced. "I've been trying to hold all the information in my brain, and sort it out into some kind of order, but all that's doing is giving me a headache." She thumped the seat with her hand. "And I feel so frustrated Melissa. We've travelled far, but in reality it feels like we're going round in circles. We get this bit of information, that bit of information, but what do we really know? Are we actually any closer to the truth, or are we on a wild goose chase?"

"Good idea, Sister," Melissa said soothingly. She was getting used to the nun's passionate outbreaks, that were so different to her otherwise headmistressy attitude. "Ready when you are."

"Good. Right. First, can you write down that on the day Jamie was murdered, I found his body at about half past three. He was last seen alive at breakfast time that day. The Cardinal immediately ordered his murder to remain secret, and you saw the Assessors enter the hostel that evening. I found Jamie's diary and discovered that he was going to disclose something to me."

Melissa dutifully scribbled away.

176

"The next day," Sister Veronica went on. "I discovered the Cardinal wanted to send me away, supposedly to keep me from talking about Jamie's death. It seems Sister Anastasia heard the murder, collapsed, and was taken into hospital. She has now died so I am unable to get any more information from the poor soul, may she rest in peace." Sister Veronica bowed her head for a moment, while Melissa continued to write.

"Father Mathers, who was party to the Cardinal's wishes about me being sent away, is now also dead. Presumed murdered," Sister Veronica's eyed flashed with darkness. "Could Cardinal Moore be Jamie's father? Is that why he is so eager to cover this up? He is an ambitious man, there's no doubt about that. A scandal that proved his lack of celibacy would certainly end his plans to progress further in the church. But I find the thought that a father could do anything so awful to his child too abominable to entertain." Or do I? She asked herself, remembering her own circumstances.

"We know from Bishop Hammett, and the Children of the Ordained team, just how rife the lack of celibacy is in the church. We know there are supporters, who want priests and nuns to be good parents while carrying on in their ministry, and we know there are the dogma enthusiasts who will seemingly do anything to keep the myth of clerical celibacy alive. Are you getting all this?"

"Yep," Melissa said. "Anything else?"

"We also now know, if Bishop Hammett is to be trusted – which I believe he is, after all what choice to we have? – That there are supporters and their foe in the highest echelons of the Vatican. And that there is much evil corruption going on too, just look at these charges of racketeering. Anything less holy, I really can't imagine." Sister Veronica shook her head.

"So it seems," she went on. "That we are fighting against a big wall of silence. They want to cover up Jamie's murder and my witnessing of the body, yet we want to bring this out into the open, and for justice to be served. For all priests' and nuns' children," she added.

*　　*　　*　　*　　*　　*　　*　　*
*　　*

Sister Veronica gave a sideways look to the nun who held the convent door open for them. The woman had quietly introduced herself as Sister Gabrielle. Previously, Sister Veronica would have automatically trusted her, but now she was wondering what her French Sister knew? What church secrets was she privy to? Since Jamie's murder her world had been turned upside down. She felt like she no longer knew anyone anymore. A person who had the title priest or nun was no longer an instinctively safe presence, if anything she felt less secure in the presence of new clergy. Nevertheless, she entered the convent respectfully and went through the appropriate greetings.

Sister Gabrielle emanated peace and reserve, and she felt her tight mental vigilance relax a little. The Sister showed them around – the small convent had originally been a medieval house. Its plain stone walls, large wooden dining table, open hearth, and surrounding rolling countryside had an instant soothing effect after the chaotic events of the previous few days. An older nun was seated in a rocking chair near the hearth. A younger one was reading at the dining table. Outside, some Sisters gardened in friendly solitude.

"Le dîner est à sept heures et demie," Sister Gabrielle said, depositing them outside their rooms before turning away. "The dinner is at half past seven."

"Thank you, Sister," Sister Veronica called after her. "I'm going to have a quick nap, Melissa. This heat is exhausting."

"Ok no problem, I'll knock for you just before dinner."

Sister Veronica had only intended to shut her eyed for a few minutes, but as soon as she lay down on the surprisingly comfy, narrow bed, she sank into a deep sleep. So it was with disorientation that she forced her eyes open, when she felt Melissa shaking her.

"Sister, Sister, it's time for dinner. Blimey, you were out cold then, I've been shaking your shoulder for a good two minutes."

All the other Sisters, and Bishop Hammett, were seated on the long wooden benches when they finally arrived downstairs; Sister Veronica's hair sticking out at wild angles.

The fish was a little dry, but it didn't matter, it was food. She wolfed it down, and accepted a second glass of wine from the old nun sitting opposite her.

A great wooziness over took her mind. She tried to reach for her glass of water, and knocked over the pepper pot. A stabbing pain shot through her stomach and she groaned, collapsing forward on to the table.

"Sister, what's wrong?" Melissa rose in alarm.

Sister Veronica could hear panicked voices in the background. Her head span, her pulse raced, and she needed to vomit. She tried to say something but her muscles wouldn't work. There was something wrong.

"What, Sister? What did you say?" Bishop Hammett was kneeling down next to her head.

"I - I – I - " Sister Veronica slurred.

"Yes?" he asked. "Try again, Sister."

"Phone an ambulance," Melissa said, taking charge. "Bishop Hammett, please help me get Sister Veronica to a bed, she needs to lie down." She wedged a shoulder under the nun's.

"The guest room is next door," Sister Gabrielle said. "Take her there."

The old nun who had served Sister Veronica the wine during dinner, watched, her face severe. Then she rose slowly and exited the room.

Sister Veronica's world was fuzzy, incoherent. Phrases from the people around her faded in and out.

"Have you called an ambulance yet?"

"Hold her, she nearly fell off the bed then."

The room was moving now, a kaleidoscope of distortions. Was she on a bed, or maybe a raft? Waves of nausea rose and fell like the tide.

"Please wait," Sister Gabrielle's voice floated above her. "I think our oldest resident, Sister Noelle -"

"No I will not bloody wait!" Melissa's voice was shrill. "My friend has collapsed and you are all standing around like idiots just watching her. Phone the fucking ambulance NOW Sister. Can't you see her life is in danger? For God's sake. My phone's in my room, can someone get it?"

A blackness swamped Sister Veronica, a welcome relief. But then fear. She was dying, she knew it now.

"Please," A thin voice, a thick French accent. "Let me give her this. I have seen these symptoms before, I think I know what has happened."

"What?"

"She has been poisoned."

Sounds of bottles being unscrewed, mixtures decanted and stirred.

"Charcoal is an antidote to many poisons," Sister Gabrielle's voice said. "Sister Noelle trained to be a doctor before receiving her calling from God. A few years ago she administered activated charcoal to a dog who ate poisoned meat and the dog survived."

"Sister Veronica is not a bloody dog," Bishop Hammett's voice. "Have you all gone mad?"

"Wait," Melissa's voice. "Look."

Sister Veronica felt a tube like object being shoved into her mouth and squeezed. Rough, old fingers pinched her lips tightly shut. She struggled, choking, a mixture of something sliding down her throat.

Time stayed still for a minute.

Then a tidal wave of nausea ripped through her body, and she was sitting up before the huge stream of sickness left her mouth, soaking the white sheet.

She opened her eyes and saw Sister Gabrielle hurrying forward with a bowl.

"You poor thing," Melissa, her make up smudged, her eyes red rimmed, stood next to the bed. Sister Veronica sank back, her limbs heavy with exhaustion.

The old nun, Sister Noelle, stood at the foot of the bed, observing.

Sister Veronica smiled weakly.

"Thank you."

Sister Noelle nodded.

"You are ok now, I think."

"Yes, you are getting some colour back," Bishop Hammett leaned forward concerned. Melissa stepped sideways away from him.

"Poison," she said. She turned towards him. "And I thought we were surrounded by friends here. Perhaps I was wrong."

Bishop Hammett stared back at Melissa.

"You can't really think I -"

"I don't know what to think." Melissa's voice was brisk, business like. "Shouldn't we call the police? Someone here has just made a very serious murder attempt."

"No," Bishop Hammett shook his head. Melissa raised her eyebrows. "The police would inform too many others in the church. It seems our whereabouts is already known by those who wish Sister harm, but if the authorities got involved they may well insist that Sister Veronica goes to hospital, and from there they may transfer her back to The Convent of the Christian Heart, where she'll be a sitting target for anyone who wants to harm her."

Melissa folded her arms.

"Look, someone just tried to kill Sister Veronica, we know that now," Bishop Hammett ran both hands through his hair. "If she'd had an allergic reaction to something in the food, the charcoal antidote wouldn't have worked. It would have only worked with poison. And no, Melissa, it wasn't me. I can see what you're thinking but I can assure you, on my life and the life of my child, that it wasn't me."

Melissa shook her head, then bent down to stroke hair away from her friend's eyes.

"Well it's too late to move anywhere tonight. I'll sleep in your room with you tonight, Sister. Then we can make plans tomorrow morning. Try and get some rest now."

Sister Veronica gave the faintest of nods.

Bishop Hammett shook his head, turned, and strode out of the room, his face unreadable.

Chapter Twenty Seven

Melissa massaged the suds into her aching head. Last night the floor had been hard, the blanket not thick enough, and she'd had a feeling she should stay "on guard" in case anyone arrived to try and inflict harm on Sister Veronica again, so sleep had been fairly non-existent. She felt uneasy being in the convent, yet she had no option but to stay. Her friend needed her, and she wasn't about to let the old lady down. She turned on the water again and let the surprisingly strong cascade drench her. If only it could really wash all her troubles away.

Drying herself and dressing, she tried to think of the bigger picture, but none came. What the fuck were they going to do? At times this journey had felt like an adventure, but now it was a living nightmare. She felt sorry she'd implied that Bishop Hammett was the perpetrator, but at the same time who else could it be? How much trust could she put in his words? Her gut instinct told her – what did her gut instinct tell her? That she had none when it came to trusting men in general. She'd actually warmed to Bishop Hammett, he had a depth of character to him that most men she knew didn't have, at least that was how he had seemed at first. But her defensive walls had come up as soon as he was under her suspicion. Why did she feel so disappointed about this? Get a grip, Melissa, she told herself. Seriously.

Stepping into the kitchen, the cooler air was a relief.

Sister Veronica smiled at her. She was sitting at the table, a cup of steaming coffee and a folded newspaper in front of her. The comforting smell of toast reached her nose, and suddenly she was hungry, ravenous.

"Please. Eat." Sister Gabrielle put a freshly buttered round of toast on the table. "Sister Veronica looks well this morning, yes?"

"Yes, thank God," Melissa slid on to the bench. "Where is Bishop Hammett?"

"Walking in the gardens. I fear he has a tortured soul, poor man," Sister Veronica sighed.

"I don't think I made his soul feel any better yesterday," Melissa said, taking a bite. "It's just that everything seemed to go out of control as soon as he arrived. I just didn't want him to hurt you, Sister. But maybe I was wrong."

"Sister Gabrielle has some information you need to hear, my dear," Sister Veronica smiled at Melissa then nodded at the French nun.

"Early this morning, I had a phone call from our contact in the Vatican," Sister Gabrielle said, walking over. "He said he has heard the name Simone mentioned in certain circles recently, and felt this might be someone in the pay of those who hold the power, someone of interest to us. Sister Veronica tells me this name means something to you all."

"Oh God, the leggy blonde secretary from Children of the Ordained."

"Indeed," Sister Veronica murmured.

"And I hear she made you all something to eat yesterday?"

"Those baguettes," Melissa closed her eyes. "Why didn't I think of that? She asked us what fillings we wanted and wrote our names on the packets. So Bishop Hammett isn't -" She looked down, shaking her head slightly. Shit. Apologizing was so cringingly difficult; you never knew how the other person would react, whether they would be cool about it or make you feel worse. Now listen, shut up and grow a pair, Melissa, she told herself. If you get things wrong, you can be woman enough to put them right. End of.

"What's that picture on the newspaper, Sister?" Melissa craned to see, eager for a temporary distraction. A dour faced man wearing a dog collar stared back.

"Ah yes, yet another sad story I fear," Sister Veronica sighed. "Sister Gabrielle, would you translate for us?"

"Of course," the nun picked up the paper. "Let's see. Yes. It says, "Police arrest paedophile priest in Lyon. Archbishop Raphael Leclercq is accused of abusing girls over a fourteen year period, during the time he was the diocesan priest in Lyon. Two of the girls claim to have given birth to Archbishop Leclercq's children at the ages of sixteen and seventeen. He *denies these allegations. Police say DNA results will confirm whether or not Archbishop Leclercq is the father."*

"It never ends, does it?" Melissa said, putting her toast down.

"What never ends?" Bishop Hammett walked through the door, his lined face more strained than ever. He was not looking much like a priest, Melissa noticed, with no dog collar, a navy chunkily knitted sweater and beige cargo trousers. It must be windy today, she thought, as his longish hair was swept back chaotically.

"Revelations about priestly transgressions and misconduct," Sister Veronica smiled sadly at him, then motioned towards the newspaper.

"Yeah, I agree. But some of us get a bad rap because of the bastards who can't behave. We are not all like that, despite current prejudice." He shot a look at Melissa.

"Ouch. But fair enough, under the circumstances. Look, I'm really sorry about yesterday," she sighed. "I shouldn't have jumped to conclusions and blamed you, it wasn't fair. I was really scared and everything seemed to be going out of control. I – I find it hard to trust men," she felt hot pink flush through her cheeks. "Maybe that was partly why I put the blame on you so quickly, Bishop Hammett. Habit."

Bishop Hammett's face softened.

"Apology accepted. And can you please all call me Chris? Bishop Hammett sounds frighteningly formal. Well if I'm off the hook, who poisoned you, Sister Veronica?"

Over tea and more toast, they filled him in on the news about Simone.

Sister Gabrielle excused herself and serenely exited the room saying she needed to prepare the chapel for prayers.

Sister Veronica took a draught of her now lukewarm coffee and stared straight ahead, not paying attention to the chatter of the other two. Well, this was a turn of events, and no mistake. She was enough of a danger to the powers that be for them to want to make her disappear for good, this much was now glaringly clear. But for the church leadership was this really all about priests' children? About hiding Jamie's murder? Killing someone was in itself evil enough for a murderer or murderers to go to great lengths to cover their tracks, especially when such a crime would contrast in the starkest terms with the apparent high morality of their profession. Priests were the messengers of Jesus Christ on earth weren't they? She chuckled darkly. Not some of them. Oh no, some came from the opposite place, the fiery depths, she knew that now. But what was all this about fake bonds? And criminal global rings within the Catholic Church? It sounded too far-fetched and ludicrous to be true. But as the memory of poor Jamie's battered body flashed into her mind yet again, suddenly fake bonds didn't seem so preposterous. Now anything seemed possible within the dark recesses of secrecy and corruption that had enveloped her life. And someone – possibly Simone, working for who? - had just tried to poison her. How had life come to this? No time for questions now, Veronica, she told herself sternly. They can come later.

What she needed was some peace and contemplation. The others didn't look up as she quietly left the room. Just the act of entering the chapel broke through the silent darkness in her head. She found a pew, the residual pain in her stomach left over from yesterday forcing her to sit rather than kneel. A calmness and joy washed through her as she closed her eyes and bowed her head in prayer.

Listen, God, source of everything, love, or whatever or whoever you are, she thought loudly. You can see what's going on here, and I can't, not yet. You can see what some people are doing in your name, the crimes they are committing, the levels of subterfuge, criminality and corruption they are prepare to go to for their own ends. Now, listen. I'm here, doing my absolute best to find justice for poor Jamie. But God, please, you have to help us now. Point us in the right direction at least. Because, quite frankly, I could do with your help.

Sister Gabrielle's words, that her contact in the Vatican had told her about Simone, floated into her mind. Was it the same contact held by Children of the Ordained? If the Vatican was the powerhouse, if it was there that decisions were made to poison, hide, make invisible, and silence people, then it was there that answers were to be found, the only place they were to be found. They must find a way to enter the lion's den. This wasn't just Jamie's fight, it was hers too, as well as many other priests' children around the world. Going to the Vatican was their best – only - chance of finding out who thought it acceptable to murder in order to publically uphold a vow of celibacy that had in reality been broken. Who thought taking a life was worth this deception, this unspeakable lie and hypocrisy. She said a silent prayer of thanks for the newly boiling blood coursing through her veins.

Chapter Twenty Eight

Cardinal Moore, having been to morning prayers in the sumptuous Sistine Chapel, now tapped a pen repeatedly against the polished wooden desktop before him. An unfamiliar uneasiness was bothering him.

He had been hoping and expecting someone to bring word overnight that the latest stage of the plan back in London was unfolding smoothly, like it always had done before. But instead Matteo, his striking blue eyes glinting angrily in a way that had made Cardinal Moore both enthralled and concerned, had arrived at 4am with the news that the interfering old nun was still active in France. Rather than a sudden bout of ill health ending her plight, it seemed – if their Parisian contact was to be believed - that she and her amassed entourage were now firmly dug in, in a miserable little convent outside Paris. Honestly, was the woman indestructible? But right now, she wasn't his main source of disquiet.

The tips of his fingers touched gently as he brought his hands together under his chin. He needed news from London. Something wasn't right, he could feel it. By his calculations, news should have reached him by now. The silence was disturbing. His hand reached out for the phone, then hesitated, as he drew it back. Then it reached out again, this time lifting the receiver and dialling the switchboard.

The switchboard was charming and archaic, both comforting and irritating. In a very plainly furnished room on the second floor of the Vatican, an army of multilingual nuns sat in grey habits answering incoming calls in mild tones. "Pronto, Vaticano" (Hello, Vatican) they repeated the phrase from 8 AM until 8 PM every day, answering more than half a million enquiries every year. They greeted all-comers with the same gentle calmness and tackled the complexity of the bureaucracy of the Roman Catholic Church with genteel grace. It was not the dedication of these nuns that Cardinal Moore questioned, they were quite rightly doing their female duty of service, more the fact but he was convinced that there was a real chance that some of them may have more than one master. Since he could not use his mobile phone signal was so intermittent here, he had no choice but to ask to be given a line. He would have to be very careful about what he said.

A male voice answered on the second ring.

"Having a lot of problems with mobile signals here at the moment, which is why I'm calling you through the switchboard," the Cardinal spoke quickly, placing heavier emphasis on the last word. There was a moment's hesitation before the voice said,

"I have heard, just now, that there's been a problem with the tea."

"I see, is this a temporary problem, or is the tea still being made?"

"I'm not sure."

"I see," Cardinal Moore said again. "Keep me informed."

"I will."

Cardinal Moore picked up the pen and tapped with renewed frenzy. And he'd been feeling so renewed, so full of zest after midnight prayers. It made the crash back to life's worries even more tiresome. Last night, just being in the same room as Cardinal Federico Pisano, the Vatican's Secretary of State and second in command to the Pope, had been thrilling. Matteo and Bishop Alfonsi had been there too, but Guglielmo, through tacit understanding, knew he was not permitted. Power dripped from Pisano, the man had such command. And Cardinal Moore knew he understood how things worked. He just got it, in a way the current Pope didn't.

"Look around," Cardinal Pisano had said to the packed chapel. "You are the chosen ones, you are special. Princes among men. God needs you and wants you to maintain the natural order of things."

There had been murmurs of agreement.

"It is a hard job for us today, my friends," Cardinal Pisano had said. "So many well-meaning people disrupt this order, they do not understand that their misplaced notions of equality actually bring chaos, and lead our world towards disaster. But we understand, don't we?"

A chorus of assent, and nodding of heads.

"We understand that God has chosen us to lead, to bring humanity to him, and to rid the world of sin. And what do we need to do to ensure this happens? We need to lead, we need to network with the most powerful in this world to safeguard our continuity, because for continuity we need resources, and above all we need to protect the holy name of the Roman Catholic Church, whatever the cost."

We *are* special, Cardinal Moore mused, as his thoughts caused some zest to return. We *are* the chosen ones. Why is that so hard for people to understand? It's what God wants. It's the natural order of things.

Chapter Twenty Nine

"Right," Sister Veronica said, walking back into the kitchen. The other two were still there, heads together, lost in deep conversation. "Now, I have been thinking," she said loudly. "And I have come to the conclusion that the only way we can progress with this any further, is by going to the Vatican."

"I've been thinking the same," Melissa's head snapped up, and Sister Veronica's sharp eyes noticed a slight flush on her cheeks.

Bishop Hammett cleared his throat and shifted position.

"Sister, if you are feeling well enough, I suggest that we leave today."

"That suits me," Sister Veronica said. "My throat is feeling much better, I think Sister Noelle's potion of honey and vinegar has really soothed it. But what is the best way to get there? Before yesterday I would have felt stupid saying this, but presumably airports and train stations would be the worst places to go at the moment, in case Vatican watchers are monitoring them."

"Hire car," Melissa said immediately. "We can book it under an assumed name and we can make sure we are not being followed."

"Yes," Chris – Bishop Hammett - nodded in agreement. "That would give us the most amount of freedom."

Sister Veronica nodded slowly.

"Let's go and pack," Melissa said. "I'll ask Sister Gabrielle to book us a taxi. I'm ready to leave this place. There was me thinking convent life was calm and peaceful but on discovery it actually turns out to be fraught with danger. I don't think it's for me after all." She laughed.

"No, I have no doubt that it is not," Chris murmured, holding out his hand as Melissa swung her long legs out from under the table.

Within the hour they were ready to go. Sister Gabrielle and Sister Noelle waved them off, and as the taxi pulled away Sister Veronica felt a pang of longing, not knowing when, if ever, she might find herself safely within convent walls again. Since her poisoning she had experienced a deep peace and tranquillity within the French convent's walls that she had not felt for a long time. And finding peace of mind was *so* important, especially when the world around her had gone mad.

They spoke little on the way to the hire car company, each one of them lost in their own thoughts. Standing in the queue for the car, she heard the Bishop say behind her,

"Aren't those uncomfortable?"

"My piercings? Nah, I'm so used to them, do you like them?"

"Well, actually, they rather suit you."

Sister Veronica thought hard. She would, she felt, have to have a quiet word with Melissa very soon.

They hired a car. As he climbed into the driver's seat, the Bishop assured the other two that he was used to long journeys, and that he had driven this exact route three years previously.

"I've been to Rome four times, actually," he turned to Melissa, who was folding herself into the front passenger seat of the Fiat Cinquecento. Sister Veronica busily spread her skirt out over the back seat. "When I'm driving in Rome I have to measure my success incrementally. The best drivers in Italy understand that they create a moving work of art – a harmonious masterpiece like the ceiling of the Sistine Chapel - with other vehicles by pressing together; the unspoken law is that the most antagonistic driver will always be awarded first place on the road. Sometimes I like to be that driver."

Melissa giggled and tucked a strand of pink and blonde hair behind her ear.

And this, Sister Veronica thought wearily as she observed the chemistry between them blossom, is why there are so many priests' children in the world. Because priests are humans, like everybody else. They fall in love, they feel attraction, they cannot tell how they will feel from one day to the next. Oh yes, I'll take a vow of celibacy, and on this precise day I one hundred percent mean it. Fast forward to sometime in the future, when loneliness has set in, or that unexpected chemical fusion has spontaneously taken place with another person, and suddenly celibacy – or perhaps chastity – is not such a straightforward concept to adhere to. So who is in the wrong, the church for having that mandatory vow, or the priests for breaking it?

She sat, lost in thought for a moment, a seething rage growing in her as dusk turned to night outside.

It's a systemic problem at the core of the Catholic church, she decided. If it were collectively possible to be celibate forever, there wouldn't be thousands of priests' children in existence, being hidden and silenced. Are all their fathers really the badly behaved black sheep of Catholicism, as they are made out to be in the press? Or is the mandatory clerical celibacy vow simply inhumane and untenable, and the solution to the unwanted children even more brutal? Welcome to the world, little baby. Your birth right is to be the living embodiment of the shame of your priest father. And a massive institution, the Catholic Church, is encouraging him to put his public – deceptive – image as a celibate priest over and above your mental and emotional health, and your right to a loving father. Hey, one day you might even be killed so that the church can continue its hypocritical public stance on celibacy. Because after all that is more important than your life. Now sleep well, and try not to feel too bad about yourself as you grow up. Oh, you've developed identity problems? Well never mind, it's just because the leadership of one of the five main global religions has discarded you as collateral damage. Haven't you worked out by now that their need for continued control and power is more important than you?

Her fingernails dug deeper and deeper into the palms of her hands until they broke the skin. Brooding thoughts continued to reel through her head and they were on the toll road to Italy before she fell into a fitful sleep.

She awoke to the sound of Bishop Hammet's hand on the horn. It was blending with hooters being deployed from all around, creating such a cacophony of noise that Sister Veronica sat bolt upright wondering if the Apocalypse had arrived. Bright sunlight gleamed through the windows, and she could see azure sky behind it. As a taxi got close to them, its wing mirror pinged off theirs.

"The thing is" Bishop Hammet was saying. "One can never hesitate here, the phrase 'he who hesitates is lost' is never so applicable as when one is behind the wheel in Rome. And there is also danger to be had in straying into areas that one shouldn't be in. For instance in the very centre of Rome there is the Varco Attivo. I once found myself there on my quest to reach the Piazza Navona."

Melissa laughed comfortably in the front.

The Bishop hit the horn again, as a truck forced them towards a car just centimetres away on the left. Sister Veronica shut her eyes.

"Did you have a good sleep, Sister?" Melissa called over her shoulder.

"Not really," came the terse reply.

"Oh no. I haven't been to sleep at all, just dozed a bit. Definitely a sunglasses day today. Bishop Hammett is taking us to a bed and breakfast he knows."

"I've stayed there before," the Bishop raised his voice above the hubbub. "Madame Romano is very helpful and accommodating. But she only has eight rooms; it's a long shot that three will be vacant but I have my fingers crossed that God will smile on us.

Madam Romano's house was a typical Rome high rise. Inside it was plain, but clean and welcoming. Sister Veronica was relieved to find three rental rooms were indeed available. She knew she needed to catch up on some sleep soon, she was starting to feel extremely irritable due to her recent lack of it. Bishop Hammett took a room on the third floor, while Melissa and Sister Veronica were given ones on second floor, where Mme Romano also slept. Half an hour later, all three sat outside the piazza near the bed and breakfast, nursing mugs of steaming black coffee, Melissa's sunglasses firmly in place.

Bishop Hammett stretched, then leaned forward.

"I have a contact in the Vatican that I'm sure that I can trust" he said. "He's not high enough to know all the workings of the Curia and the top leadership, but he is a sympathetic ear. You see, he and I have one very important thing in common. We are both fathers." He blinked as he said the last four words.

"You acknowledge your child, at least in private," Sister Veronica could hear the bitterness in her own voice. "You are a part of her life, you love her and are trying to be a father and a priest. I can see how this torments you, but you should be proud that you are trying."

"I could not love my daughter more, the thought of disowning her, of not seeing her would be too painful for me to bear. I don't understand those who can do this." His eyes moistened. "I often grapple with this conflicting situation I find myself in. I have a child who I love and who I would never change, yet I feel so guilty for this. I promised celibacy and I failed that promise, yet my daughter has brought me more joy than anything. Why is it so hard?"

"It shouldn't have to be," Melissa said, her eyes narrowing. "Personally, I think the whole thing's bullshit. Sorry Sister, but I do. A man has a child. Big deal. Why make him and the

206

child feel so guilty? Other ministers have families, in the Protestant and other faiths, and it doesn't make them any less effective at their jobs. In fact it probably makes them more effective as they will be able to understand family life more. Catholicism is starting to seem like a big cult to me; separate from your families, disown your children, follow our dogma or be shunned."

They finished their coffee in silence.

Bishop Hammett shook himself, stretched and stood up.

"Sister, are you up to walking to the Vatican, it's not too far?"

"Yes, yes, the fresh air might wake me up a bit."

They set off through streets crowded with tourists and other men and women of the cloth.

"Vatican City is never quiet," Bishop Hammett said, as they walked. "Everyone who visits Rome wants to see the Vatican at least once. Luckily, as we are 'family' we will not have to follow the normal tourist route."

They walked through ancient courtyards, across a large square, approaching a door where they were admitted after

Bishop Hammett showed them his ID. They passed offices, and large rooms with their doors open through which they could see ornate meeting tables. Eventually they reached a modest looking office, where Bishop Hammett knocked on the door. There was a shuffling behind the door before it was swung open by priest, who ushered them inside. Bishop Hammett made the introductions.

"We cannot speak here," the priest, introduced as Father Bianchi, said. "Let's go to the gardens. If we walk and talk it will appear to onlookers that I am showing you around."

Filing out of the small office, they followed Father Bianchi to the gardens that turned out to be beautifully tended; full of fountains, sacred sites, and views that made Sister Veronica stop and stare. Passing through several small curated gardens including one comprising solely of cacti, Father Bianchi pointed out a small collection of olive trees. What a truly marvellous harmony between professional gardening and natures wonders, Sister Veronica mused. This was something exciting, being here in Rome. Much as recent events had tainted and changed her belief in the Catholic Church, being somewhere so magisterial was breath-taking. From almost every spot they could see St Peter's dome, an omnipresent reminder of whose gardens they were in. She couldn't help noting that the beautiful architecture of the dome signposted the power and all-consuming control that had not only shaped the gardens, but the lives of those who lived in the dome's shadow.

As they reached a small fountain with ornately decorated walls flanked by a sculpted figure, Father Bianchi stopped and motioned towards two benches either side of a small pond. Tiny turtles swam appeared as the group seated themselves.

"I have been working with the office in Paris and have now identified the father of the young man, Jamie, who so cruelly had his life taken from him," Sister Veronica nodded. She loved it when people got straight to the point.

"Can you tell us who it is?" Bishop Hammett said.

"I can," the priest said. "I wish it wasn't true, I believe this man is probably well known to you already. His name is -"

"Father Bianchi!" Loud staccato tones cut across the priest. Sister Veronica looked round at the approaching figure in red.

"Father Bianchi. Something has happened and Archbishop Canci wishes to see you in his office this instant."

"But -"

"This *instant*. Go now. Do not worry, I will continue the tour with these good people."

Shooting Bishop Hammett a desperate look, Father Bianchi stood up and walked off. And there we have it, Sister Veronica thought. Roman Catholic power and control, all siphoned through hierarchy, in action.

They had no choice but to walk with the man, who introduced himself as Bishop Alfonsi, as he headed back towards the dome. Sister Veronica had the distinct impression that they were being herded. Dash it all, they'd been caught so soon. She heard Melissa curse under her breath.

Bishop Alfonsi nodded towards a gate.

"We'll go this way. I take it Father Bianchi has not yet shown you the front of St Peter's Basilica?"

"No, he didn't have a chance," Sister Veronica said loudly.

She followed the others through the gate, lingering exhaustion slowing her down, and suddenly they were surrounded by people again. A man was walking towards her, carrying two disposable cups balanced on top of each other. He turned to look behind him as he passed. Try as she might to side step out of the way, the man marched straight into her, and as he did so dark brown liquid shot out of the cups, drenching her shirt and skirt. The smell of coffee beans saturated her senses.

"Oddio, mi dispiace." The man raised his hands to his face. "Prego, scusi. Please, excuse me, I so sorry."

"Watch what you're doing." Bishop Alfonsi's voice was back to staccato. "You are soaked, Sister. This will never do. Please, come with me and I will find someone to help."

The man, now holding empty containers, backed away, still apologising.

Bishop Alfonsi took Sister Veronica's arm and guided her towards a smaller building to the left of St Peter's.

"Please, go inside and have a look round. We won't be long," he called to Melissa and Bishop Hammett.

Sister Veronica tried to shake her arm free but Bishop Alfonsi's grip was vice-like.

"Come with me," she mouthed to Melissa and Bishop Hammett, but as she turned she saw two men step out of the crowd and block her friends' way; try as they might, they could not pass them. She heard Melissa yell loudly.

Bishop Alfonsi half guided, half dragged her through the small building's entrance, that had a large "No Entry" sign above it, all the time wearing a look of important superiority on his face. Guiding her firmly in front of him, he followed her into the dark space, shutting the door firmly behind himself, then bolting it. He pushed her on through the room, his hands vice-like on her arms, through a series of doors and corridors, through rooms progressively less magnificent and more shadowy than the previous. They finally came to a halt in a room with no windows. The only light came from a stained-glass panel above the door.

Sister Veronica felt a cold rush of rage.

"What exactly do you think you're doing?"

"Just keeping you safe, Sister. Safe from meddling any further in things you don't understand."

"I really wouldn't do that if I were you," Sister Veronica spoke quietly.

"Oh really? And why's that?"

Sister Veronica considered the man's arrogant face. There was no warmth in his eyes at all. What would appeal to him? What drives him to believe he is so special?

"Because God would not want one of his prince's to act in such a way."

Bishop Alfonsi's eyes narrowed.

"You, a mere woman, dare to tell me what God wants?" His voice was smooth, steady. "And how would you know, Sister? Do you have a special hotline to the Lord? Are you closer to him than his apostles?"

Sister Veronica hesitated. Right, so he was a misogynist as well as a deluded bully. He must have detected scepticism on her face as he smiled.

"Ah, I see you do believe this. You are there to serve, Sister. That is all. Service is an important role, you should have stuck to it. But you felt you were more important than this didn't you? You felt you knew better than Cardinal Moore, you chose to involve yourself in matters meant for men to deal with. You are nothing but a deluded fantasist, Sister. Your actions have disgraced you and harmed many, including God the Almighty. I am here to remind you of your place. It is for your own good. Did you really think you would get away with bringing shame on our beloved church?"

"Our beloved church?" Sister Veronica repeated, thoughts whirring fast through her head. What would be the best angle to take with this man?

"You're right, Your Eminence," she said, casting her eyes downwards. "I realised my mistake days ago, and I have been praying hard for forgiveness ever since. I will be obedient from now on, I promise."

"Do you think I'm a fool, Sister?"

"No, Your Eminence. Not at all."

"Yet you expect me to believe you have had a sudden change of heart, a sudden epiphany? Do you think I'm as foolish as you, woman?" A shadow of a smirk crossed Bishop Alfonsi's face. "Now I have more important things to attend to, but my two friends here will take good care of you." He motioned to the darkness behind Sister Veronica. She heard chairs scraping, and footsteps. Two men emerged from the shadows; one look at them told her they were definitely not priests. Their eyes were cold and watchful. One walked towards her, fists full of cable ties, as the Bishop slid open the bolts and left, closing the door behind him. The other bolted the door, and pulled a ragged piece of material out of his pocket.

A shiver of fear coursed down Sister Veronica's spine as the men pushed her backwards onto a chair. Pressing her arms down, they bound them to the sides of the chair with the cable ties, then did the same with her legs. One man shoved the dirty rag into her mouth, and the other roughly applied tape over the top. They stopped to survey their work, then apparently satisfied they retreated back into the darkness. Sister Veronica could hear one of them muttering in Italian. The other laughed in reply, an eerie, cruel sound that sent a chill of fear through her.

Try as she might, she could not move. Pain seared through her arms and legs at the points where the ties cut into her flesh.

Breathe slowly, Veronica, she tried to sooth herself. Keep the airways clear. But it was too much, and as panic overtook her, silent tears streamed from her eyes. Well, God, she shouted. I'm in your hands now.

Chapter Thirty

Cardinal Moore looked up. Someone was knocking quietly on the door.

"Come in," he said. Bishop Alfonsi entered, drawing up a chair on the opposite side of the desk.

"Did you manage to secure the artefact we were looking for?"

Bishop Alfonsi gave a slight nod, a hint of a smile playing on his lips.

"Yes, the artefact is being stored in a location that is very discreet with no likelihood of being discovered."

"Very good." Cardinal Moore's shoulders relaxed as he breathed out. "And what of the charitable donation to the UK? Has that been delivered yet?"

"The donation was received ten minutes ago," the Bishop gave another ghostly smile.

"What was the delay?"

"It was a minor problem, now neutralised."

Chapter Thirty One

"Non capisco," the policeman kept repeating. "Non capisco, I don't understand." He glanced at the two men, suctioned to Melissa and Bishop Hammett's side, who rewarded him with satisfied nods.

"No, you don't understand. Listen to what I am saying," Melissa's pulse raced out of control. "Someone has taken our friend. They went through that door over there and didn't come out. Please help us. Just go and investigate, please."

"They are all in it together," Bishop Hammett muttered under his breath. "Watch their eye contact."

"Well we are truly fucked then, aren't we?" Melissa's voice rose as her arms shook, fear taking her over. "If the police are in on it, who are we supposed to ask for help? Sister Veronica is in danger, they tried to kill her yesterday. What if they've already -" She stopped, unable to finish the

217

sentence, the words too awful to even say. She looked down at the ground, head spinning, running on empty, out of ideas.

Bishop Hammett forced himself to take a deep, slow breath.

"Don't give them the satisfaction of seeing you distressed," he said in a low voice. "Let's move away from these people and think about what to do next."

He took her hand and led her away. Melissa could feel the eyes of the three men searing into her back.

"They're still watching us," she muttered.

"Ignore them. Its run Mafia-style here, always has been. But we still have the free will to think and talk. Let's stand here, where they can't see us." He looked at her white face. "Do you want to sit down for a minute? I think you might be in shock."

Melissa nodded. Still holding his hand, she slid down the wall into a crouching position, willing her thoughts to stop reeling.

"What are we going to do?" She whispered. "God knows what they're doing to her. The police are corrupt. We're being watched. There's nowhere left to turn. Oh God, poor Sister Veronica." Unspeakable images of what could be happening to the nun flashed through her mind. Tears began to leak from her eyes. "I'm scared we might never see her again."

Bishop Hammett took out his phone.

"I'm going to call Father Bianchi," he said.

Chapter Thirty Two

Sister Veronica woke up with her cheek pressed against her shoulder. Pulling her head upright was downright torture, the muscles had contorted and Saints knew how long she'd been out for. Fear was exhausting, she could remember her eyes closing, she could remember welcoming the darkness as it washed over her, eliminating the terror.

As she stirred, rushes of pins and needles shot down her arms and legs so she stayed still for a moment, orientating herself, willing her blood to pump effectively to those areas that needed it. Thank goodness she'd fallen asleep. Her brain was sharper now, more alert.

Her eyes grew accustomed to the near darkness. Sister Veronica craned to hear noises, breathing, anything that would identify the presence of her captors; but she heard nothing. Had they gone? It was hard to tell.

Minutes – or perhaps hours – passed; time was a fluid void. Her face felt tight and pinched where the strong tape pulled at the flesh. There was no point moving her arms and legs, the resulting pain was too much to bear. Have faith, Veronica, she told herself. There are more forces at work in this world than we can comprehend, don't assume the worst will happen. And if it does, it's not the end. You know it's not. Death is a door to pass through, not a finality.

Primal fear kept rearing its snake-like head, and for unidentifiable amounts of time her head whirled with terror. But horror would not win, she was sure of that. So she played her favourite hymns and Christmas Carols round in her brain until each time the panic subsided.

Her stomach growled and ached. And she desperately needed to empty her bladder. Drat, damn and double blasted hell.

The on-going silence in the room must mean the men were either asleep or absent. She tried making some muffled noises out loud, and still there was no hint of additional human presence.

Then a sound, a metallic fumbling from the dark recesses of the room, like someone was trying to open an internal door. Instantly, adrenalin flooded back through her veins and her skin bristled.

Hurried footsteps approaching, then,

"Oh Sister Veronica, what have they done to you?"

It was Father Bianchi's voice. Feeling a surge of gladness as his distraught face came into view, Sister Veronica sent a heartfelt prayer of thanks to the cosmos. Father Bianchi peeled away the tape from her mouth, and removed the rag, shaking his head, tears at the corners of his eyes.

"We don't have much time," he whispered, bending down to untie her arms and legs. "Are you OK, Sister? What did they do to you?"

"Oh I'll live," Sister Veronica flexed her aching arms. "Bishop Alfonsi was here. He kindly left two thugs to take care of me, they were the ones who tied me up."

221

"The Bishop is a wicked man," Father Bianchi muttered. "The thugs are groundsmen here, they have gone outside to smoke cigarettes. They are clearly in his pay. So much corruption exists here, in this *holy* place. Bishop Hammett called me but I couldn't answer, as too many people were near me. So instead I received a text from him about what happened to you. I know these rooms very well, when he told me the door you were taken through I thought they would bring you here, to the depths of the labyrinth, it's so soundproof and unused. I've been watching and waiting for an hour. There, all done. Can you stand up, Sister? Here, give me your hands and I will help you."

"Yes, its fine, I can walk," Sister Veronica said, as she stood up slowly. Apart from the searing pain in her calves where the cable ties had left their mark, her legs worked well.

"Quick, we must hurry. Here, take these papers, Sister. If anything happens to me again, it's important you have them. They contain the information you are looking for." Father Bianchi withdrew a fold of documents from his pockets, and thrust them at Sister Veronica, who swiftly deposited them in her deep pockets.

"Thank you," she said, following him as he turned towards the darkness at the back of the room. "Really. You've saved my life."

"I'm glad," Father Bianchi whispered. "Now follow me. We must not talk now. We must go this way and hope we make it. Too many watchers are at the front of the building."

They reached the door, and Father Bianchi pushed it open.

A man stood there. For a split second Sister Veronica wondered if she was imagining things, but she recognised his scarred face immediately – one of her captors.

"Ciao," he said, holding up a knife.

"Run, Sister," Father Bianchi shouted, grabbing the man's arm, twisting the knife away. "Go, go now!"

Sister Veronica hesitated.

"GO!" Roared Father Bianchi, squirming as the thug bent the knife back towards his throat.

She went, running into the darkness, sending up a prayer of protection for her rescuer, then flinching as she heard Father Bianchi cry out. On and on, feeling the walls on either side of her. There was a door here, was it safe to open it?

She didn't know, couldn't tell. So she ran on, further into the blackness, until she hit a wall. Her fingers fumbled, trying to read what was in front of her. Another door, a fastened bolt. Her fingers shaking, she slid back the bolt and found a stairwell before her, bathed in murky light. She had no option, she knew, she must go down the stair to whatever fate awaited her.

The light came from grills in the walls. A cold, damp smell reminded her of her grandfather's cellar. At the bottom of the stairs was a room full of stacked chairs, rows of folded tables, broken statues and piles of boxes, all grey and eerie in the dim light. A door, again bolted. She grabbed an old piece of material that covered a fractured mirror and threw it over her head, an ad hoc headscarf would have to do, she needed some sort of disguise. Pushing the papers even further down in her pocket, she drew the bolts back and stepped outside, her head bowed, the mildewed material swinging round her shoulders.

Finding herself in a distinctly less magnificent courtyard than those on display in the Vatican Gardens, Sister Veronica walked past piles of cigarette butts, listening to washing machines whir behind nearby walls. The murmur and hubbub of the crowds got louder, and through a gap between two buildings she spied a group of Japanese tourists, cameras at the ready.

Inching forward, headscarf pulled closely around her face, Sister Veronica surveyed the scene in front of St Peter's Basilica. She saw the henchmen that had deterred Melissa and Bishop Hammett from following her. They had their backs to her, and were clearly staring at something. Daring herself to poke her head round the corner, she saw their visual targets; Melissa, white and drawn, next to Bishop Hammett, who was talking frantically into his phone.

Compulsively patting the papers in her pocket again, Sister Veronica felt a hard lump at the bottom. A pen. She always carried one, never knew when she would need it. And thank goodness for that. Drawing it out, she carefully took out the folded papers, and tore off a strip of blank white at the bottom of the last page. Much as she yearned to read their contents, the documents would have to wait until later.

Meet me at the car, she wrote in capital letters, before folding the paper up and depositing the rest of the stash deeply back in her pocket.

Retracing her steps to the storage room she had exited the building from, she fished around and collected a bundle of drapes and rags that covered other old items, quickly folding them into a rough pile. Rearranging her headscarf into the most convincing style she could manage, with a good deal covering her face, Sister Veronica picked up her pile of materials, her folded note clutched tightly in one fist. You're a washerwoman, she told herself. You work here. Don't keep looking around, don't look guilty. Just look straight ahead.

Stooping slightly, and adopting a limping gait, she came once again to the gap between the buildings.

Right, Veronica. Into the lions' den.

Thirty Three

The British Vatican contact exited The Wessex Building Society and immediately became anonymous in suburban London's insalubrious Hounslow High Street. His phone rang.

"Yes?"

"Is it all safe?"

"Oh very safe indeed. The tea has not only been made but poured successfully and handed out."

"Excellent."

"Has the other problem been cleared up?" The British contact cleared his throat. It puzzled him as to why this particular clean-up had taken so long. If he'd been there…

"I believe so."

"Very good."

"God bless."

"God bless, Father."

Chapter Thirty Four

Melissa stared straight ahead, listening to Chris talking to Dominique.

"Yes we know it was Simone," he was saying, turning away and staring out at the gardens. "Bloody traitor. No, we don't know where Sister Veronica has been taken. We have our own spies watching us, we can't get near the buildings, we've tried. Yes, I've phoned and texted Father Bianchi but he hasn't replied yet. They are watching him too."

An old woman hobbled towards them, carrying a pile of washing that didn't look very clean at all. Melissa observed her limp past their watchful guards, heading for a nearby gate. As she came closer, the old woman lifted her head.

Sister Veronica! Thank bloody God, she's still alive.

Careful not to change her facial expression in anyway, Melissa turned towards the dome, squinting. A smell of musty material wafted past as Sister Veronica shuffled on, and Melissa felt the gentlest tap on her shoe. Glancing down, she saw a fold of paper had landed there. She waited a few minutes, still pretending to scrutinize the dome of St Peter's, before getting her notebook out of her pocket, pretending to fumble with it, and dropping it next to her feet. Bending down, she retrieved not only the notebook, but the folded paper.

Meet me at the car, she read.

Good work, Sister, ten out of ten for acting ability, you old superstar.

Heart pounding, Melissa withdrew her phone from her pocket, thanking her lucky stars that she had decided to ask Chris for his number the day before.

Don't ask me any questions now but we need to get back to the car, she texted him. Sister Veronica's going to meet us there. I'll explain everything on the way.

"Ok, ok, I'll let you know if anything changes, Dominique," he was saying. "Yes I agree, this is all a nightmare. Right, stay in touch, bye for now."

"Received any new texts?" Melissa murmured.

Chris looked down at his phone, then put it in his pocket.

"There doesn't seem to be any point in us staying around here," he said. "What do you think?"

The two men looked interested, one took a step forward.

"No, I think you're right," Melissa sighed. "I'm so tired. Shall we go back to the bed and breakfast for a bit?"

"Good idea," Chris took her trembling hand, and led her out through the gate.

They're following us, Melissa thought, as Sister Veronica's back view disappeared into a side street. The footsteps behind them got louder and closer.

Chapter Thirty Five

Cardinal Moore, basking in the praise of the special committee – SB9, set up to investigate the ordained involved in the clerical abuse scandal – found Bishop Alfonsi's entrance rather unwelcome. Those who sat on the council were handpicked by the Pope to give him advice and guidance on critical matters that related to the future of the Catholic Church. The Pope had given instructions to SB9 that he wanted help in identifying any Cardinals that the council may do better without. Two Cardinals including the one investigated by Cardinal Moore had been written to and thanked for their service and a third Cardinal had also been dismissed by his Holiness and although age may have been the explanation given, it was widely known that the decision to dismiss had been due to far more than just advancing years. The highest ranking prelate whose name had been linked with a sex scandal abroad had been granted an indefinite leave of absence, and Cardinal Moore had his eyes firmly set on the opportunity that his superior's time off presented. He was very pleased with the outcome of his investigation. He had handled it in the delicate manner that was required, and had done an excellent job. He felt that at last he was being appreciated for the skills he possessed. He had even had a hand written note from the Pope himself, expressing his gratitude. He was important, a prince.

"My apologies, but Cardinal Moore is urgently needed," Bishop Alfonsi's voice was smooth but his eyes dripped with darkness.

"Of course," the elderly Cardinal in charge smiled benignly and waved his hand.

Cardinal Moore sighed, then stood up.

"She's gone," Bishop Alfonsi spat, when they were alone in the corridor.

"What? But that's impossible?"

"Father Bianchi went in to release her when Gioele and Filippo went out for a cigarette. He told me he needed to go to the bathroom but he never came back, he must have worked out where she was being held and went straight there. Gioele returned in time to find them leaving, but

Father Bianchi apprehended him, and ended up getting stabbed. He's now fighting for his life in hospital, I don't expect him to last the night. We immediately minimized the scandal of course, explained to the police that Gioele went mad and stabbed him and that he must be suffering from a mental illness. He's now in custody."

"That woman is dangerous," Cardinal Moore growled. "She knows too much about the death of Jamie Markham. She needs to be stopped. As you know it's not just about Jamie, it's about protecting our financial source in Britain. There's too much at stake here."

"Yes, I know, we understand that," Bishop Alfonsi muttered. "But she's proving difficult to hold."

"Next time, don't hold her. Finish the business once and for all immediately. Understood?"

"Yes, Your Eminence. It will be done. And this time she will be made to suffer greatly for the inconvenience she has caused."

To be continued….

Printed in Great Britain
by Amazon

41452502R00139